THE RUNAWAY SUMMER

By the same author:

THE SECRET PASSAGE

ON THE RUN

THE WHITE HORSE GANG

A HANDFUL OF THIEVES

THE WITCH'S DAUGHTER

SQUIB

CARRIE'S WAR

THE PEPPERMINT PIG

REBEL ON A ROCK

THE ROBBERS

KEPT IN THE DARK

For older children:

DEVIL BY THE SEA

THE RUNAWAY SUMMER

by

NINA BAWDEN

LONDON
VICTOR GOLLANCZ LTD
1982

© Nina Bawden 1969

First published September 1969

Second impression April 1971

Third impression September 1972

Fourth impression February 1976

Fifth impression June 1980

Sixth impression November 1982

ISBN 0 575 00337 5

Printed in Great Britain by
St Edmundsbury Press, Bury St Edmunds, Suffolk

For Charlotte Sington, and Perdita Kark
With love

Contents

ONE

'I wish I could do something really *bad* . . .'

MARY WAS ANGRY. She had been angry for ages: she couldn't remember when she had last felt nice. Sometimes she was angry for a good reason—when someone tried to make her do something she didn't want to do—but most of the time she was angry for no reason at all. She just woke in the morning feeling cross and miserable and as if she wanted to kick or break things.

Aunt Alice could make her angry just by being there, with her rabbity face and grey hair in a bun and the little tuft of spiky beard on her chin that waggled when she talked; and her teeth that made a clicking sound at mealtimes, and her stomach that sometimes made a noise in between—a watery suck and gurgle like the last of the bath running out. And when *she* tried to make Mary do something she didn't want to do, it made Mary so cross that she grew hot inside.

This morning, Aunt Alice wanted Mary to wear her woollen vest. It was such a lovely July day, with the wind blowing and the small clouds scudding, that Mary had been in a better mood than usual when she came down to breakfast. She had even eaten her porridge because she knew her grandfather believed it was good for her. When he saw her empty plate, he had beamed over his newspaper and said, 'Well, it looks as if our good sea air is giving you an appetite at last,' and seemed so pleased, as if in eating a plateful of porridge

Mary had done something quite remarkably good and clever, that she wondered what else she could do. She thought she might say, 'I think I'll go down to the sea and skim stones after breakfast,' because she knew this would please her grandfather too: he worried when she did what he called 'moping indoors.'

And now Aunt Alice had spoiled everything by asking Mary if she had put on her woollen vest!

'That jersey's not thick enough for this treacherous weather,' she said, looking nervously at the window as if the weather were a dangerous dog that might suddenly jump through it and bite her.

Mary scowled and felt her face go solid and lumpy like a badly made pudding.

'It's not cold,' she said. 'And I'm hot *now*. If I put my vest on, I'll be boiling to *death*.'

'There's quite a wind out. It's blowing up cold. I know I'm wearing *my* vest! Just between you and me and the gatepost!'

Mary looked carefully round the room. 'I don't see any gatepost,' she said.

Aunt Alice laughed in her high, silly way—not as if she were amused, but as if she were trying to apologise for something.

'It's just an expression, dear. Haven't you heard it before?'

'I've *heard* it all right, but I think it sounds potty,' Mary said. 'And I just *hate* those horrible old vests. They've got sleeves! Sleeves and *buttons!* I expect you knew I'd hate them, that's why you bought them for me!'

She stabbed her spoon into her boiled egg, and some of the yolk spattered out.

'Oh Mary,' Aunt Alice said in a sad, fading voice. Pale

eyes bulging, nose twitching, she looked like a frightened rabbit.

Mary knew her Aunt was frightened of her, and this made her more bad tempered than ever. It was so ridiculous for an old woman to be frightened of an eleven year old girl.

She said bitterly, 'No one else in the *whole world* wears vests with sleeves and buttons.'

Aunt Alice said, 'Oh Mary,' again. She sounded as if she were trying not to cry. Grandfather put down his newspaper and looked at her. Then he smiled at Mary.

'My dear child, someone must wear them or the shops wouldn't stock them, would they? It's a case of supply and demand. No demand, no supply.'

For a second, Mary almost smiled back at him. It was, indeed, quite difficult *not* to smile at her grandfather, who looked, with his round, rosy face, and round, blue eyes, rather like a cheerful, if elderly, baby. He was bald as a baby, too—balder than most, in fact: the top of his head was smooth and shiny as if Aunt Alice polished it every day when she polished the dining room table. Usually, just to look at her grandfather made Mary feel nicer—a bit less cross, certainly— but now, after that first second, she felt worse, not better, because she saw that his blue eyes were puzzled and that he was playing with his right ear, folding the top over with his finger and stroking the back with his thumb. This was some- thing he only did when he was thinking hard or worried about something, and Mary knew he was upset because she had been rude to Aunt Alice. Although this made her ashamed and miserable underneath, it made her angry on top.

She said, 'But children don't buy their own clothes, do they? They just have to wear what grown-ups buy for them, horrid, prickly old vests and beastly *skirts* if they're girls. They don't have any say, they just have to do what they're *told*.'

A lump came into her throat at this dreadful thought and she swallowed hard and glared at Aunt Alice.

'Children don't have any say in anything. They have to wear what they're told and eat what they're given and . . . and . . . live where they're *put*. It's not *fair*.'

The lump seemed to have gone from her throat and settled on her chest, like a stone.

Aunt Alice made a funny noise, midway between a gasp and a sigh.

Grandfather said, 'Mary, since you don't seem to want any more to eat, perhaps you'd like to leave the table and go upstairs for a while.'

He spoke gently and reasonably, as he always did, whatever Mary had said or done. Sometimes she wished he would shout at her instead: his being so nice, made her feel nastier, somehow.

She got down from her chair and left the room without another word, but as soon as she had closed the door, she stopped to listen. She knew that people always talked about you, once you had gone.

'Oh Father, it's all my fault.'

'Nonsense, Alice.'

'Of course it is!' Aunt Alice sounded crisp, almost indignant. She liked to think things were her fault, even things that couldn't possibly be, like bad weather or a train not running to time. 'I just can't manage the poor child,' she said. 'I blame myself.'

'I know you do. I wish you wouldn't.' Grandfather spoke quite sharply for him. 'Alice my dear, try not to worry. It's natural that Mary should be a bit difficult, in the circumstances. She'll settle down, given time. She's a good child, underneath.'

Mary gritted her teeth and stumped upstairs. She wasn't

good underneath. She was bad. She was so bad that everyone hated her except her grandfather, and he only didn't hate her because he was differently made from other people and didn't hate anyone.

Mary went into her bedroom and scowled at herself in the looking glass. '*I* hate you, too,' she said, aloud. 'Pig.' She doubled her fists on either side of her jaw and pushed up the tip of her nose with her little fingers so that the nostrils showed. Now you even *look* like a pig! An ugly, horrible pig.'

'Oh, I wouldn't say that. Only when you pull that face at yourself.'

Mary turned and saw Mrs Carver, who came to help Aunt Alice in the house on Wednesday and Friday mornings. She was a little, thin woman with a thin, pale face that looked thinner and paler than perhaps it actually was, because it had so much red hair frizzed out all round it.

Mary said crossly, 'You shouldn't come into people's rooms without knocking. It's rude.'

'You're a fine one to say what's rude and what isn't.' Mrs Carver grinned, showing big, square teeth that seemed too big for her face, rather as her hair was bright for it. 'I was going to make your bed. You can give me a hand, since you're here.'

'Why should I? It's your job, you're paid for it,' Mary said, and then caught her breath. This was really a very rude thing to say, and she knew that red-headed people were supposed to be quick tempered.

But Mrs Carver only looked amused. 'True,' she said, and twitched off the bedclothes. In spite of being so thin and small, she seemed strong and very energetic, darting round the room in a series of short, sharp rushes, rather like a terrier; snatching at blankets, picking up Mary's clothes. Mary stood by the window and watched her. When the room was tidy, Mrs

Carver said, 'Your Auntie was talking about having the room painted up for you. What colour do you fancy?'

Mary looked out at the garden, not answering.

'Come on, now,' Mrs Carver said. 'You must have some idea. What about a nice yellow? Would you like that? Your Auntie wants you to have a colour you'd like.'

'She can paint the room black if she likes,' Mary said. 'I don't care. I shan't be here long.'

'Won't you?'

Mary said quickly, 'My mother's gone on holiday and my father's had to go to South America, on business. He's gone to Chile.'

'I know.' There was a funny look on Mrs Carver's face, as if she knew something else, too. Something that Mary didn't know. She decided that she hated Mrs Carver.

She said, 'I don't suppose *you* know where Chile is!'

'I went to school once.'

Although Mrs Carver smiled as she said this, Mary could see she was beginning to be angry.

'*Well*, then.' Mary tossed her head. 'If you know where Chile is, you know it's a long way away, don't you? And costs a lot of money to get there. So he couldn't take me, and I had to come and stay with stupid old Aunt Alice. But as soon as he gets back, he'll come and fetch me straightaway.'

Mrs Carver's face had pinched up during this speech and now looked paler than ever, as if all its colour had drained into her hair. 'If you were my little girl, I wouldn't be in too much of a hurry,' she said.

'I'm glad you're not! I should just *hate* to be your little girl, I should hate to be anything to do with you *at all*.'

Mary's heart was thumping as if it had suddenly come loose and was banging about in her chest. She ran out of the bedroom, across the landing and into the bathroom. She locked the door. She heard Mrs Carver rattle the knob, and then her voice, calling softly as if she didn't want anyone else to hear. 'Mary. Mary, dear ... ' but Mary sat on the edge of the bath and stared in front of her, and after a minute, Mrs Carver went away.

Mary stood up and pulled faces at herself in the bathroom mirror until she felt better. Then she unlocked the door very quietly, crept across the landing, and went down the stairs. Aunt Alice was in the kitchen, singing, 'Eternal Father, strong to save, Whose arm doth rule the restless wave.' She had a light, trembly voice that wobbled on the high notes.

Mary opened the back door, which had blue and red stained glass panels, and went into the garden. It was a big garden, with a lonely, dark, tangled shrubbery all round it, and what Aunt Alice called a 'nice tidy bit' in the middle, where there was a lawn and flower beds cut in neat shapes. Grandfather was standing on the lawn and looking at a rose bed. He always said he was fond of gardening, though it seemed to Mary that he really meant he liked standing and looking at things growing while Aunt Alice did the weeding. But all the same, he had special clothes for gardening which he was wearing now: an old check jacket that was too big for him, since he had shrunk up as he had got older, and a woolly hat Aunt Alice had knitted out of odds and ends of bright wool, with a fat, red bobble on top.

When Mary came up to him, he smiled as if nothing out of the ordinary had happened at breakfast, and said, 'Hallo, there. Come to give me a hand in the garden?'

Mary said, 'Grampy, when am I going home?'

She hadn't meant to say this. The words just came out, as if there was someone else inside her, speaking them.

Grandfather looked at her. There was a funny look on his face as there had been on Mrs Carver's—as if they both knew something Mary didn't—but there was a sort of sadness mixed up with it, as if Grandfather were sorrier about whatever-it-was than Mrs Carver had been.

He said, 'Don't you like it here?'

Mary wriggled her shoulders and sucked at a strand of hair as if she found this a difficult question to answer, though in fact it shouldn't have been, and not only because it was pleasant to live near the sea instead of in London, and have a garden to play in, and a shrubbery where she could be private when she wanted to be, and light fires and make camps. Mary was fond of her grandfather—as fond as she was of anyone, that is—and he and Aunt Alice were always at home and never left her by herself in the evenings as her father and mother sometimes did, with only a bad-tempered black cat for company. This cat was called Noakes; he had a raggedy ear and a blind eye, both scars from old battles, and he bit and scratched whenever Mary tried to stroke him. She didn't blame him, because she knew how he felt, being shut up in a stuffy flat when he longed to be out, roaming the streets and fighting other cats, but there had been times when she wished he would curl up on her bed and purr, instead of crouching resentfully on the window sill and glaring with his one, good eye. Mary wasn't frightened of being left alone, indeed, she wasn't frightened of anything very much (she was a little like Noakes in that way as she was in some other ways too) but she had often been bored, and, since she had been staying with her grandfather, she had found it was comforting to hear voices downstairs when you were lying awake in bed. Particularly when you knew that these voices would never get loud and shout at each other.

In fact, Mary could have said, with absolute truth, 'Yes, I do like being here.' But she always found it hard to say she liked anything, just as she found it almost impossible to say 'Thank you,' or 'I'm sorry.' Sometimes she wanted to, but the words stuck in her throat, like pills. So all she said was, 'Oh, it's all right, I suppose.'

Grandfather prodded a weed with his walking stick. 'You know, Aunt Alice and I like having you. Very much indeed.'

Since Mary knew this could not be true, she scowled and said nothing.

Grandfather said, 'Of course, it's natural you should miss your Mum and Dad.'

'Oh, I don't miss *them*.' Mary was so surprised that he should think this, that she spoke quite naturally for once. Then she saw the look on her grandfather's face and knew that it was the wrong thing to have said: nice children always missed their parents when they were away from them. She looked away and muttered, 'Always quarrelling and banging doors.'

Grandfather cleared his throat. 'Well, your friends, then. You must miss your friends.'

'I didn't have any.' Mary thought for a moment. Grandfather clearly wanted her to miss somebody. 'I suppose I miss Noakes a bit. My cat.'

'I remember.' Grandfather chuckled. 'He once bit me. Right through my trousers. Drew blood. I suppose we could have him here if you really wanted, though your Aunt isn't very fond of cats.'

'Oh, Noakes isn't an *ordinary* cat,' Mary said. 'He's more of a wild cat, really. He once killed a ginger tom, a *huge* one, *twice* his size, and he's driven hundreds of others away. The people in the other flats are always complaining.'

'I don't think Alice would like that,' Grandfather said. 'She prefers to be on good terms with the neighbours. But you can have some kind of pet, I daresay. Not a dog, perhaps. Alice was once bitten by a dog.'

'I wouldn't mind an alligator,' Mary said hopefully. 'We had a baby-sitter once when I was younger, who had an alligator called James, and she kept it in her bathroom.'

'I was really thinking of something a bit less exotic,' Grandfather said. 'A rabbit, say. I used to keep rabbits when I was a boy.'

Mary shook her head. 'Rabbits are boring.' She thought her grandfather looked disappointed, so she went on, 'It's all right. I don't really want a pet. I don't even want to go home, really. It's just that I want to know when I *am* going.'

Her grandfather poked in the rose bed with his stick and found another weed. 'I don't know.' He looked at her sadly. 'I'm sorry, Mary.'

She stared at the rose bushes. 'You mean they're not coming back for me?'

Grandfather was making patterns in the earth with his stick. Mary looked at his hand, holding it, and saw there were veins on the back, like blue worms. He said, 'Well, nothing has been decided.'

Mary's mouth had dried up. It felt rough and furry. She said, 'They're getting a divorce, aren't they?' and knew, suddenly, that she had known this all along—for weeks now, ever since the middle of June when her mother had brought her to stay with Grandfather and Aunt Alice—but saying it out loud made it seem worse, somehow.

Grandfather's ears were red as the red bobble on his woollen hat and his face had gone sagging and crumpled. He looked

so unhappy that Mary wished she could think of something
to say to cheer him up, but she couldn't think of anything.

He said, 'My poor child, I'm afraid they are.'

That, *my poor child*, made Mary feel very odd. She usually
hated it when people seemed to be sorry for her, but her
grandfather had spoken so gently and lovingly—as if she
really was *his* poor child, and he cared how she felt and
what happened to her—that it almost made her want to
cry.

She didn't; Mary hardly ever cried, even when she hurt
herself badly. She just said, in a flat, bored voice, 'They don't
love me, then.'

'What nonsense. Of course they do.' Grandfather sounded
shocked and Mary pulled a face, but turned away so that
he shouldn't see. She might have known he would say that!
Grown-ups were all the same: they said things, not because
they believed they were true, but because they thought
they ought to be. 'They both love you very much,' Grandfather said. 'It's just that—well—just that they don't love
each other, anymore . . . ' He sighed a little. 'Of course,
your mother was only eighteen when she married. Just a child.
A silly, pretty child.'

He half-smiled, as if he was thinking of Mary's mother
when she had been a girl. Then his smile went, and he sighed
again, and said that the trouble was, people changed as they
got older, and sometimes—not always, but sometimes—if
they had married when they were very young, they grew
apart. They couldn't help this. It was just something that
happened. No one's fault.

Mary stopped listening. There was no point. Her grandfather was so good-natured that he never thought anything
was anyone's fault.

She stared straight in front of her and froze into a statue. She often did this when something unpleasant was happening: stood quite still, unfocused her eyes into a blue, and held her breath, so that she not only looked like a statue, but if she tried really hard, could almost believe she *was* one, stony-cold and feeling nothing. She could still hear things, people talking and moving about, but what they said or did seemed to be nothing to do with her.

She knew Aunt Alice was in the garden because she heard her, talking in a low, agitated voice to her grandfather, and his calmer voice, replying, but she didn't look at them, or move, not one frozen muscle, until Aunt Alice touched her shoulder and said, 'Mary. Oh Mary, darling . . . '

Then Mary came alive, turning from a statue into an angry, red-faced demon, whirling round, fists clenched, so that Aunt Alice stepped backwards as if she were afraid Mary might hit her. 'Don't call me darling, don't you *dare* . . . '

'Darling,' was what her mother and father called her. *Mary darling, Darling Mary.* As if they loved her.

'I hate being called darling, it's just soppy,' Mary shouted, and ran off across the lawn, so fast that her cheeks jolted, into the shrubbery.

She threw herself on the ground. Although she shut her eyes she could still see her grandfather's bewildered old face, and Aunt Alice's silly, rabbity one, bouncing up and down. She rolled over and over, grinding her teeth and scrabbling her fingers into the soft, leafy earth. She hated herself. She was horrible, that's why her mother and father left her—Mrs Carver had as good as said so—and now she had been horrible to grandfather and Aunt Alice. Aunt Alice was a silly fool with hairs on her chin and a rumbling stomach, and she said silly things like, *between you and me and the gatepost*, and *Tell it not in Gath!* but she only meant to be kind, and Mary had been horrible to her. And what was worse—so much worse, that Mary felt as if she could hardly bear it—was that neither Grandfather nor Aunt Alice would blame her or get angry. 'Poor Mary,' they would say, 'she can't help it.'

Whatever she did.

'Poor Mary,' Mary said in a disgusted voice. Then, 'Damn. Damn and *hell.*' She pulled up loose handfuls of soil and leaves and rubbed them over her head and face. Some of the earth got in her mouth, which stopped her. She sat up, grimacing and spitting and said, aloud, 'Oh I wish . . . I wish I could do something really *bad.*'

TWO

Stop Thief!

MARY RAN. SHE ran out of the garden, through the main street of the town, and along the sea front, towards the pier. Her head thumped, and when she breathed, the air hurt her teeth and stabbed down her throat, like a knife.

The wind was so cold. The early morning sun had gone (as Aunt Alice had guessed it might) and the beach was almost empty; a shingly shelf sloping down to a wide, shining expanse of blue mud, with gulls crying over it.

And not only the beach was deserted. Most of the cafes on the promenade were boarded up and the Fun Fair was closed. There were very few summer visitors this year, because of the tar on the beach, and the only people in sight were very old; pensioners, sitting wrapped in scarves and overcoats in the shelters on the front, and looking out to sea as if they were waiting for something.

As she passed one of the shelters, Mary put two fingers in her mouth and gave a sudden, loud whistle, but none of the old people jumped. They didn't even look at her. Only a few gulls rose, startled and screaming.

Mary hunched her shoulders and walked on. Just before the pier, there was an open kiosk that sold sweets and ice-cream and buckets and spades and enormous, cotton-wool sticks of candy floss. Outside the kiosk was a large, stuffed bear; if you put sixpence in the box round his neck you could sit on top

of him to have your photograph taken. Usually Mary thought
he looked alarmingly realistic, with his grinning, red mouth,
and spiky, yellow teeth, but today, with no one on his back,
he looked forlorn and moth-eaten—indeed, there was quite
a large hole in his side with some of the stuffing showing
through. Mary prodded her finger into the hole and pulled
out some of the kapok fluff, and the man in the kiosk poked
out his head and shouted at her.

Mary stuck out her tongue, and jumped off the promenade
on to the beach, beside a small jetty. On the other side, there
was a patch of sand where two small children were playing,
building a castle and decorating it with seaweed and lumps
of tar. Mary heaved herself up on the jetty, lay on her front
on its green, slimy surface, and looked down at them. When
they saw her, she pulled a face. She could pull awful faces,
and this was her best one: her mad face, which she made by
pulling the corners of her mouth up and the corners of her
eyes down with her thumbs and forefingers, and, at the same
time, pressing the end of her nose with her little fingers so
that the holes of her nostrils showed. She knew that if she
rolled her eyes as well, this could be very frightening, and
it did frighten the children. They burst into tears, and stumbled,
howling, along the beach to their mother who was snoozing
in a deck chair. She opened one eye and said, '*Now* what's the
matter with you?'

Pleased with this success, Mary scrambled off the jetty and
ran further along the beach, past the pier to the bathing huts.
But there were no more children in sight, only a woman
sitting in the shelter of one of the huts. She was wearing an
ancient fur coat—more bare patches than fur—and she had
an old, lined, papery face, but when Mary pulled the mad
face at her, she jumped up with surprising agility, shook a

rolled-up newspaper at Mary and said, 'Go away this minute,
you rude, naughty child.'

'Go away this minute, go away this minute,' Mary chanted,
copying the old lady's indignant voice and waving her hands
about, but inwardly she felt cast down. 'Naughty' was a
babyish word. Only small children were naughty. She pulled
another face—as if she were going to be sick—but her heart
wasn't in it, and the old lady just looked contemptuous. She
sat down, arranged the mangy fur over her thin knees, and
closed her eyes.

Mary watched her. Sometimes it upset people if they opened
their eyes and knew you had been staring at them all the time.
But the old lady stayed so still that she might really have
been asleep—or dead—and after a minute Mary gave up
and climbed the steps on to the promenade. She felt, suddenly,
heavy and lumpish, and so bored that she wanted to yawn.
Pulling faces and annoying people was too easy, there was
nothing *to* it! If Grandfather knew, he wouldn't even be
cross! He might say 'Well, dear, it wasn't very kind, was it?'
But that would be all!

Ordinary naughtiness was no use, then. Mary didn't really
know what she meant by 'no use'; just that she wanted to do
something much worse, so that Grandfather—and everyone
else—would know how really bad she was. She felt that in
some queer way this might make her feel better.

But what could she do? She looked at the desolate promenade and the long line of shuttered bathing huts. Grandfather
rented one of these huts to change in when he swam, which
he did every day, when it was warm enough. Aunt Alice
thought he was too old to swim, now he was nearly eighty
years old, and was always telling him so. He might have
a heart attack, or drown, or catch a cold! Aunt Alice couldn't

do anything about the heart attack, or the drowning, since she had always been too frightened to learn to swim herself, but she did her best to prevent his catching cold by coming down to the hut with him and making him cocoa on the stove inside. Grandfather hated cocoa, but Aunt Alice made him drink it, standing over him with a Do-as-I-tell-you-or-else, expression.

Mary thought that old people were often no better off than children, with other grown-ups always bullying them and knowing what was best for them and making them wear vests and drink cocoa.

She thought of a way to get her own back on Aunt Alice. The key to their bathing hut was hidden underneath, fastened to the bottom step by a piece of wire. She could get inside and make a good mess—empty out the sugar on to the floor and put sand in the cocoa . . .

For a minute, the idea seemed a good one, then she found herself yawning. She felt too lazy to go to all that trouble! Besides, Aunt Alice was short-sighted. She might not notice the sand in the cocoa, and Grandfather would have to drink it! And even if he found out whose fault it was, he would still only say, 'Poor Mary. It's not her fault she's naughty. She's upset and you can hardly blame her.' (Since people were always making excuses for Mary and she was always listening at doors, she knew just what he would say.)

Mary yawned again, until her jaw cracked. No—if she was going to do something bad, she would have to think of something worse than that. Something *criminal*—like being a bank robber or a murderer!

She began to walk back towards the pier, jumping the cracked paving stones and crossing her eyes to make it more difficult. Then she wondered how long she could keep her eyes crossed and concentrated hard on this, succeeding so well that a passing woman glanced at her, averted her own eyes hastily, and said to her husband, 'What a terrible tragedy! Such a pretty child, too!'

By the time Mary got to the pier, her eyes ached with squinting and she felt hungry. Finding half a crown in her pocket, she went to the kiosk for a stick of candy floss. She wondered if the man would recognise her as the girl who had been pulling the stuffing out of his bear, but he didn't really look at her; he gazed at a point somewhere beyond her shoulder and served a man who wanted a packet of cigarettes, although Mary had been there before him.

Mary hated the man in the kiosk for this. When he finally attended to her, giving her the candy floss and turning to the till for change, she took two Crunchie Bars from the front of the counter and put them in her pocket. She took her change, smiling so brightly, and saying *thank you* so pleasantly, that the man seemed startled. He smiled back and said it was a pity it had blown up so cold, after such a fine morning.

The Crunchie Bars were sticking through the stuff of her jeans. Mary kept her hand over the bump and backed away from the kiosk, still smiling hard. Then she turned and skipped off, humming under her breath. She felt excited and scared at the same time. She longed to look round to see if there was anyone around who could have seen her, but she didn't dare. She went on, hopping and skipping and humming like a girl without a care in the world until she came to some steps that led to the beach. She ran down them, jumping the last three, on to the shingle.

Her heart was thumping. She crouched in the shelter of the sea wall which had a concrete lip, curving over her head. The sea came right up, during high tide, and it smelt seaweedy and sour close to the wall, rather like the smell in a cave. Mary wrinkled her nose, but didn't dare to move. Alarming fears were crowding in on her, making her legs feel stiff and heavy. Suppose someone had seen her! Suppose hundreds of people had seen her! She had thought the sea front was empty, but suppose all these people had really been hiding—in the shelters and behind the bandstand, and under the tall, wooden legs of the pier! Waiting and watching! Suppose they had all risen up and run after her, shouting together, 'Stop thief, stop thief . . .'

Suppose they were running after her *now*.

Her heart thumped faster. When someone actually spoke, she thought it would jump right out of her throat.

'We seed you,' the voice said. It came from above her head.

Mary dropped her candy floss. Looking up, she saw two faces looking down. Small, red, round faces that seemed, for a dreadful moment, to be fastened directly on to the top of two pairs of very short, stumpy, red legs. Then she saw that these nightmarish creatures were in fact two quite ordinary children, crouching on their haunches on the lip of the promenade and peering down, their chins resting on their knees. They wore shorts and had close-cropped, dark hair, slicked down so flat that it might have been painted on their heads.

'We seed you,' one of the children repeated, and giggled.

'T'isn't *seed*, silly, it's sawd,' said the other, and giggled even louder, fat cheeks puffing up like small, shiny balloons. 'We sawd you,' it gasped in a hoarse, triumphant voice, 'Pinching.'

This last word was not really very loud, the child was giggling too hard, but it seemed loud to Mary.

'Ssh . . .' she hissed, but they went on, laughing helplessly, nudging each other and falling about, until she said, savagely, 'Fat-faced snigger-poufs. Shut up and go away.'

They stopped giggling at once and looked astonished, as if no one had spoken so unkindly to them before. Then the corners of their mouths turned down and Mary was terrified that they would begin to cry. She couldn't see over the lip of the promenade, but the children were only little—not more than five or six—so it was likely that there was a grown-up somewhere, looking after them. And if they cried, the grown-up would come hurrying up . . .

Mary had forgotten that she wanted everyone to know how wicked she was.

She said, as gently as she could manage, 'I'm sorry, I didn't mean to be horrid, but you are a pair of *sillies*. I didn't pinch anything. That was a *silly* thing to say.'

They looked at each other. They were exactly alike: the same shining brown eyes, the same licked-down hair. And now the same stubborn look settled on both their faces.

One of them said, 'But we was watching. We seed.'

'We *sawd* you,' the other corrected.

'You don't say seed *or* sawd. You say saw. We *saw*.' Mary spoke impatiently. She had no brothers or sisters and had forgotten how easy it was to make mistakes when you were small. Then she remembered that grammar wasn't exactly important at this moment, and went on, hastily, 'But you didn't. You didn't see anything because there wasn't anything to see! I just bought some floss and two Crunchies, and now the floss is all spoiled because you made me jump.' She pretended to be more upset about this than she actually was, kicking the floss with her toe and grinding it into the shingle. 'Look at it! Shrinking up already and covered in muck!'

They both looked so guilty, their eyes meeting hers and then sliding miserably away, that she felt sorry.

She smiled to cheer them up. 'Never mind. You didn't mean it, did you?'

But their faces remained solemn and sad. One of them said, 'I've got a mint in my pocket. It's a bit hairy, but you c'n have it if you like.'

'Poll don't like mints. I ate mine,' said the other.

'I'm like Poll, then,' Mary said. 'I don't like mints much. But I tell you what, if you come down here, I'll give you a bit of my Crunchie Bar.'

Once they were on the beach, they would be safely out of sight of whoever was looking after them. She could give them a Crunchie and then escape! Their legs were short and the stone steps were steep: she could be up and gone before they got back on to the promenade.

They shook their heads.

'We've got our clean shorts on to go to the dentist.'

Mary kept her smile fixed. It was no good getting cross. She said coaxingly, 'Well, you won't get them dirty if you're careful. And anyway, the dentist wants to look at your teeth, not your bottoms.'

This made them giggle. Then they looked at each other.

'Come on, I haven't got all day,' Mary said. She took one of the bars out of her pocket and began to peel off the gold paper, not looking at them. She heard them whispering and then the slip-slap of their sandals as they ran to the steps. They were very slow, coming down one behind the other and one step at a time. Mary felt sick and shivery as if she were going to the dentist too. She thought that if she ate a Crunchie herself, she would probably *be* sick.

They came stumbling along the beach, their eyes shiny and hopeful. She stripped the second bar and said, 'Look, one each! Aren't you lucky!'

Two fat hands shot out. Mary wondered which was Poll, and if their own mother could tell them apart.

Guessing, she said, 'Here you are, Poll,' but she was wrong. The little girl grinned through a mouthful of Crunchie. 'I'm not Poll. I'm Annabel. Anna for short. People always get mixed.'

'S'ever so funny at school,' Poll said.

They looked at each other, chocolate dribbling from the sides of their mouths.

'I once blowed in my milk and Poll got put in the corner,' Annabel said.

Poll giggled. 'Then the teacher found out, and she gave me a lemon drop.'

Mary thought they were really rather sweet, with their funny, round faces, and blobby noses, and gruff little voices.

'Watch out, Poll, you're getting chocolate on your jersey,' she said.

Poll looked down, her chin disappearing into several other chins as she did so. 'Oh Polly-wobble, you mucky pup,' she said, sounding so comic that Mary laughed.

Or began to laugh, rather. What stopped her—stopped her dead, so that she stood there with her mouth hanging foolishly open—was someone calling above her.

'Pollyanna, Pollyanna . . .' As if the twins were one person.

She whispered to them, 'Look, I've got to go . . .' but before she could move a boy had appeared at the top of the steps.

'Pollyanna!' He was down the steps and lurching along the beach, a heavy shopping bag dragging him down one side and banging against his leg. 'I *told* you not to go on the beach. *And* what are you eating?' He sounded less like a boy than a scolding grown-up, though he wasn't, Mary thought, much older than she was. A bit taller, perhaps, and thinner, with a worried, freckled face and gingery hair. '*Sweets!*' he said in an ominous voice.

'She give us them,' Poll said.

He put down the shopping bag and rubbed his hand against his trousers. 'You're not supposed to take sweets from people, Mum's always telling you . . .' He looked at Mary and said, his voice still grown up, but apologetic now, 'I'm awfully sorry, have they been bothering you?'

'Oh, they weren't *her* sweets, she stole them,' one of the twins said. Which one, Mary didn't know, because their voices were so alike and she wasn't looking at them but at the boy, who began to blush. The blush rose from the collar of his open-necked blue shirt and covered his face, until it was almost the same colour as his hair.

'That's a lie.' Mary was trembling. She stood with her back against the sea wall and pressed her hands against it, to steady herself.

The boy said, 'Pollyanna!' and both little girls looked at him, innocent and wide-eyed.

'We *sawd* her, Simon,' Annabel said. 'She bought some floss, and we watched her do that, then she took the other sweeties while the man wasn't looking.'

'I paid for them though. Lying little kids.'

Though Mary spoke contemptuously, she wished a hole would open in the sea wall and she could vanish into it. Or that she knew some special word to make her invisible. In the fairy stories she had read when she was little, something like that always happened, when things became too hard to bear, and although Mary didn't read that sort of story now, and thought that fairies and magic were just a lot of rubbish, she couldn't help scratching with her fingers in the slime of the

sea wall and hoping, with half her mind, that she would find
some sort of knob or button . . .

But nothing happened. She just went on standing there,
with the grey sky overhead and the sliding shingle under her
feet, and the twins and this embarrassed boy, watching her.
He was still blushing. He said, 'You shouldn't say that.
They don't tell lies. They may be little, but they don't tell
lies.'

'Lying's worse'n stealing,' Poll said smugly, finishing her
Crunchie and wiping her hands all over her front.

'Look what you're doing!' Mary said, hoping to divert the
boy's attention. He was supposed, wasn't he, to be looking
after Poll and Annabel, and stop them getting dirty? But it
was no use. He just glanced briefly at Poll and said it couldn't
be helped now. And anyway, chocolate washed out easily,
not like tar.

Then he turned back to Mary. He had blue-green eyes with
brown flecks in them, like pebbles. Mary noticed people's
eyes. She had found that she could often tell from them what
they were thinking—which was sometimes quite different from
what they said.

But this boy's eyes baffled her. They were puzzled and, in a
funny way, sorry. Mary couldn't think why he should be
sorry for her.

He said, 'Were you hungry?'

This was so unexpected that Mary didn't reply.

His face had gone red again. 'I just thought you might have
been.'

Annabel was clutching at his sleeve. 'Please Simon, let's have
a Trial. We oughter have a Trial.'

Poll jumped up and down. 'Please Simon. *I* c'n be a Witness
and *she* can be the Prisoner in the Dock.'

'*I* want to be a Witness,' Annabel said. 'I never been a Witness, not in my whole life. It's not fair.'

Mary stared at them.

Simon said, 'It's a thing we do at home sometimes, when someone's been naughty and won't own up . . .' He looked embarrassed, as anyone might, having to explain a private family custom to a stranger, but there was something else in his expression as well; a kind of shyness, or shame. He turned on the twins and muttered, 'It isn't a *game*. Can't you see, she's a poor, hungry girl? I don't suppose she had any breakfast this morning.'

Poll said, 'I ate up *my* breakfast. I had cornflakes and eggy toast and milk and an apple.'

'Shut up,' Simon said, very fiercely, and she blinked and put her thumb in her mouth.

Mary, who had been holding her breath, let it out in a long, rushing sigh. *Of course*. Before she had come down to the sea she had rolled in the dirt in the shrubbery and rubbed it all over her face and into her hair. Some of the leaves and earth would have blown out in the wind, but she must still look like some kind of tramp or gipsy. Someone terribly poor . . .

That was why Simon was sorry for her.

For a moment, this seemed a terrible insult and she wanted to shout that it wasn't true; even if she wasn't rich herself, her father and mother were. Rich enough, anyway, to buy her as many old Crunchie Bars as she wanted.

But she didn't say anything. She opened her mouth, looked at Simon, and shut it again. She was afraid, she suddenly realised, not of anything he could *do*—she could run away from him quite easily, since he was lumbered with Polly-Anna and the shopping basket—but of what he might *think*.

That she should mind about this, rather surprised her.

Usually she didn't care a fig what people thought about her, except for a few special people like her grandfather, and a teacher she had once had called Miss Phipps, who had been extra kind when she first went to school. And there was nothing obviously special about Simon.

She hung her head and watched him through her lashes. He was just a thin, sandy boy, with eyes like speckly pebbles. Very ordinary to look at, and yet she knew—or felt, rather, because since she had just met him it couldn't be a matter of knowing—that he was a person to be reckoned with. All she really knew was that she would rather he was sorry for her, than he should despise her.

Poll said, 'Didn't you really have any breakfast? Not even cornflakes?'

Mary shook her head. Her long hair flew across her face and hid it.

'Why didn't your Mummy give you some?' Annabel said.

'Or your Dad?' Poll added. 'Our Dad gets breakfast Sundays and when our Mum's in bed having a baby. She had one last week so he got breakfast this morning and we done the shopping.'

'I don't live with my mother. I live with my Aunt,' Mary said.

'Why didn't your Auntie give you some then?'

'Why don't you live with your Mummy?'

The twins spoke together, solemn eyes fixed on Mary; two solid, determined little girls who liked to get to the bottom of things. They were like steam-rollers, *nothing* would stop them, Mary thought, and glanced at Simon for help, but he had his back to her, bending over the shopping basket.

'My Aunt don't care if I have breakfast or not!' Mary knew that this was a bit hard on Aunt Alice who cared desperately, convinced that Mary would die of starvation if she left so much as a half slice of toast or a spoonful of egg, but it was the only explanation she could think of at the moment. As for the other question, it was too embarrassing to answer truthfully, and she couldn't think how else to answer it, so she pretended it hadn't been asked. She walked down the beach, picked up a handful of stones, and began to throw them at an old tin can, half buried in the shingle.

'Perhaps her Mummy's dead,' Poll whispered behind her.

'*Is* your Mummy dead?' Annabel asked, coming up and peering into her face.

'Mind your own business.' Mary threw another stone at the can. It missed and she said 'Damn,' very loudly.

'You shouldn't say that word, it's rude,' Annabel said in a reproachful voice. 'And you shouldn't be rude. I was only asking. And I was asking *nicely.*'

Mary felt trapped and frantic. 'All right then, *yes.* Yes, yes, *yes.* She's dead.' She felt, suddenly, quite hollow inside. She glared at the little girl. 'In fact, my father is, too. I'm an orphan. Anything else you want to know?'

Annabel shook her head. She ran away, up the beach to Simon and Poll. Mary knew they were all whispering about her. She went on, throwing stones and missing the can, because her eyes had blurred over. Perhaps if she took no notice of them, they would go away.

But Simon said, beside her, 'I've got something. I mean, if you're hungry . . .'

He was holding a chunky sandwich.

'Sardines. I bought some for our tea, so I opened a tin and made a sandwich.'

Mary had never felt less hungry in her life. And she hated sardines.

Simon was looking wretchedly shy. 'I'm sorry there isn't any butter.'

Mary took the sandwich. She hadn't meant to: her hand seemed to move of its own accord. She bit at it apprehensively and was not comforted: it tasted quite as nasty as she had feared.

The twins had come up behind Simon and were standing on either side of him, gazing at her. Suddenly Annabel said, 'Manners!' She spoke in a loud, stern voice.

'*Ssh* . . .' Simon said, at once. He turned on his sisters. 'Clear off now. Quick sharp. Up the steps.'

They protested, 'She oughter say *something*,' and, 'You're always telling us about Manners, it's not *fair*,' but they went obediently enough.

Simon apologised. 'I'm sorry, they're only little.'

'No. It's my fault.' Mary swallowed a lump of bread and sardine and said, quite humbly, 'I should have said thank you.'

'I expect you were just too hungry. It must be awful . . .'

He looked, and sounded, so troubled, that Mary couldn't laugh. Besides, she had the horrible feeling that he intended to stand there watching her eat, as if it were feeding time at the Zoo.

She said, 'I can't eat it all at once. When you're really hungry, it's best to eat slowly. If you don't, it can be quite dangerous. It's the shock to the stomach.'

He looked doubtful for a moment, then his face cleared and he grinned at her. 'It's all right. I'm not staying.'

But he didn't go, either. His grin faded and he shifted from one foot to the other, looking uncomfortable. Finally he said, in a rush, 'I say, it's none of my business, but I suppose you will get some dinner? I mean, is your Aunt dreadfully poor?'

'Of course she's not poor,' Mary said, without thinking.

She saw the surprise on his face and added, hastily, 'And she doesn't starve me, *actually*. It's just that she—she doesn't like me, so she gives me scraps and left-overs, and they're not always nice.'

'Why doesn't she like you?'

Inwardly, Mary sighed a little. She enjoyed making up stories about herself, but she liked to have time to get them properly worked out before she told them to other people. And Simon hadn't given her time, she thought indignantly. He was as bad as his sisters, poking and prying . . .

She tossed her head. 'Curiosity killed the cat!'

Simon went red—he blushed very easily, just like a silly girl, Mary thought—but he spoke quite calmly. 'Oh, all right. I'm sure I don't want to know.'

He started up the beach. Mary watched him—and felt lonely. He was a horrid, inquisitive boy, but he was the first person of her own age she had spoken to for over a month. Neither Grandfather nor Aunt Alice knew any children. Grandfather's friends were all old, and Aunt Alice was too shy to have any. She talked to her neighbours but only when she had to: most of the time she pretended not to see them, when she passed them in the street.

Mary struggled with herself. Then she called after Simon. 'I'm sorry.'

He stopped and looked back. His face was blank.

She said, 'I didn't mean to be foul. It's just that . . .' Just what? Her mind seemed empty; then words came into it and she used them. 'Just that I don't really want to talk about it.'

'All right.' He sounded off-hand, as if he were still rather hurt, but he did smile at her. 'It's a bit silly. I don't even know your name.'

'Mary.'

'Well. I'm Simon Trumpet.' He paused. 'Look—I mean—well—if you . . .' His voice tailed away; he bent over the shopping basket and heaved it up, leaning sideways to take its weight, and then said, as if he had picked up his courage with it, 'I mean, if you get hungry again, you could come to tea, or something. We live at Harbour View, just beyond the pier.'

He didn't wait for an answer. He ran up the steps and Poll and Annabel closed on him, one taking his free hand, the other holding the basket.

They were out of Mary's sight almost at once, but she waited five minutes by her watch before burying the remains of the sardine sandwich in the shingle. Then she began to work things out in her mind. She might not see Simon again, but if she did, she intended to have a good story ready.

THREE

The Boy from the Sea

'MY AUNT DOESN'T like me. She's only looking after me because of the money. My father was a rich man, you see, almost a millionaire . . .'

Mary was sitting on the beach and talking to herself; no sound, just her lips moving. Now she stopped and frowned. Her father was a business man; he made quite a lot of money, but Mary wasn't sure how. All she really knew was that he travelled a lot and this was one of the things her mother was always complaining about. Mary stared at the sea which was slowly creeping in now, across the shiny mud, and wondered what her father could have been that would sound con- vincingly rich . . .

'He was a Bank Manager,' she said, at last. 'And when he died, he left all his money to me, though I don't get it until I'm twenty one. If I die before that, the money goes to my Aunt, so she hopes I *will* die, of course. She doesn't dare starve me, and she's not really cruel—if she beat me, the bruises would show and the neighbours might notice! But it's pretty scarey sometimes, especially if I get ill, because I know what she's thinking. I had a cold last week and she sent me to bed and took my temperature. She said it was normal but I knew it wasn't because she looked so pleased! And all that day and the next, she made me stay in bed and she kept coming in, and when- ever I woke up, she was there in the room, watching me . . .'

Mary felt excited and shivery. She could almost believe this was true, as to some extent it was, of course: she *had* had a cold last week and Aunt Alice *had* made her stay in bed. She had said that colds often flew to the chest at this time of year.

The clock at the end of the pier struck a quarter to one, and Mary left the beach and made for home. She talked to herself all the way, enlarging on Aunt Alice's wickedness and adding a few details to make it sound more true. She decided that Aunt Alice must be her father's sister and not her mother's, so that she would be more likely to inherit the money if Mary died . . .

By the time she had washed her hands and was sitting at the table, Mary was so pleased with the way the story was going that she ate an enormous lunch, quite without thinking. Aunt Alice, who had been worrying about her all morning, was greatly relieved. When Mary passed up her plate for a second helping of rice pudding, Aunt Alice looked as happy as if someone had given her an unexpected present. Mary tried not to look at her: she was busy describing Aunt Alice as a horrible creature with a long nose and black, beady eyes, and the sight of her Aunt's mild face, beaming with pleasure, was a little confusing. 'Of course she *looks* kind,' she said silently, 'but it's all put on so that no one will guess . . .'

Grandfather said, 'Were you trying to say something, Mary?'

'No, Grampy.' Mary looked at him innocently. It was hard to talk to herself without moving her lips just a little, but she did her best. 'Of course, my grandfather's not unkind, but he's dreadfully old and doesn't notice much. He's going blind, too, so he doesn't see when she takes all the nice meat out of the stew and only gives me a spoonful of fat and gristle . . .'

'Are you sure, Mary?' Grandfather's sharp eyes were fixed on her. They looked puzzled.

'Perhaps she's been taught that little girls should be seen and not heard,' Aunt Alice said brightly.

Mary gave her a scornful look. 'Of course it's not *that*. I was just telling myself a story!'

'Was it a good one?'

'Oh, *very*,' Mary said, trying not to giggle. 'Can I get down now?'

Grandfather and Aunt Alice smiled at each other. Then they both smiled at Mary. The room was full of sunlight.

'Of course you can, dear.' Aunt Alice was so happy because Mary had eaten her lunch that she looked almost pretty. 'What do you want to do this afternoon? We could go for a walk in the park . . .'

'That would be nice,' Mary said, speaking extra politely because this was the last thing she wanted to do. The park was full of old ladies and their dogs. 'The trouble is, I promised to meet some friends on the beach. I played with them this morning, and they said they'd be there this afternoon.'

Aunt Alice looked anxious. 'I hope they're nice children, dear. Not rough.'

'I don't suppose she's taken up with a gang of desperadoes,' Grandfather said.

'No.' But Aunt Alice still sounded doubtful. 'You know the tide's in, this afternoon, and the beach can really be quite dangerous, in places . . .'

Mary fidgeted. Her head was bursting with ideas about her wicked Aunt and her blind and feeble grandfather and she longed to be alone to get on with them. She said, 'It's all right. We built a sandcastle this morning, and we thought we'd collect shells this afternoon.'

She thought that not even Aunt Alice could think these were dangerous occupations, and she was right: her Aunt smiled and said, well then, as long as she was *careful*. But Mary must remember not to go near the jetty when the sea was fully up because a boy had been drowned there, last year. And she must look both ways crossing the road and *never* speak to strange men . . .

Mary had heard these warnings so often that she could have repeated them word for word, but she said, 'Yes, I'll be very careful, Aunt Alice,' in a tone of such unnatural pleasantness that her grandfather glanced at her in some surprise.

In fact, Mary was a little surprised herself. As she ran down to the sea, she thought that perhaps she had only been nice to Aunt Alice, to make up for being so nasty about her, in her mind.

She said to herself, 'She's got a bottle marked POISON in the cupboard. It's a blue bottle and it's hard to see how much there is in it, unless you hold it up to the light. It's about half full now, and every time I go past and she's not there, I try to look. If it gets emptier, then I'll have to be careful because I'll know there might be some in my food. I'm careful about that, anyway. If we all have something out of the same dish, like potatoes or stew, then I know it's all right. But if we have something she brings in on separate plates, then I mess it about and leave it, just in case . . .'

She wondered if Simon would believe this. She thought he might be rather a difficult person to convince. Not that it mattered, because she probably wouldn't see him again, and didn't, indeed, particularly want to.

He was such a bossy boy. Besides, he knew she had pinched those Crunchie Bars.

The thought made Mary uncomfortable. She began to whistle loudly, to take her mind off it.

The weather had changed again: it was much warmer now and the sky was blue. The tide was right in but the wind had dropped and there were no waves on the water which moved against the sea wall as gently and soundlessly as water tipping in a cup.

Mary walked to the pier and beyond, where there was a line of tall, terrace houses. They had names like Sea Vista and Water's Edge. Mary sauntered past them, whistling softly, and trying to look as if she wasn't looking.

Harbour View was the last but one. It was shabbier than the others, badly needing a coat of paint; and instead of a neat front garden with flower beds and paving, it had only a worn, trodden patch of grass. A playpen stood in the middle with a happy, fat baby in it, hanging on to the sides and gurgling. It had thrown all its toys out of the playpen, adding to the litter already on the lawn: a tricycle on its side, a tennis racket with half the strings missing, two dustbins and a punctured beach ball. Beside the step that led up to the front door, there was an old pram with the hood up. As Mary watched, the baby inside began to cry and the front door opened. A little woman with grizzly hair came hurrying down the steps, and Mary turned and ran.

She ran until she was puffed, suddenly horrified by the thought that Simon might have been looking out of a window and seen her. She would hate him to think she had come to look for him!

She made for her grandfather's bathing hut. The weather had been bad since she came, and this was the first time since last summer that she had been there. But the key was where she remembered, on its piece of wire, and after fiddling with the rusty padlock for a little, she pulled the creaky door open. Inside, the hut smelt cold and shut-up: she crinkled her nose and pushed the door wide, to let in the clean, salty air. Everything was neat and in its place: there was sugar in the tin marked sugar, and tea in the tin marked tea. There was even a hook on the wall for Mary's bucket and spade, and two boxes on the table, one for the shells and one for the stones that Mary had collected last year. There were sparkly stones and dull, blue ones, and others with strange, knobby shapes that the sea had made. Mary turned the stones out, remembering the feel of some and the look of others. It struck her that while most grown-ups would have kept the shells, they would almost certainly have thrown away the stones when they cleared up the hut for the winter, and she wondered if Aunt Alice liked keeping things, as she did herself: her old toys, even the shoes and the clothes she had grown out of. It was a habit that annoyed her mother. *Oh, for heaven's sake, Mary, this isn't a junk shop. What on earth do you want to keep all that rubbish for?*

Mary squatted on the step of the hut and let the stones dribble slowly through her fingers.

'My Aunt's thrown most of my toys away,' she said. 'She's kept a few locked up, but she only lets me play with them when the solicitor who looks after my money comes to see her. Then she gives me the toys, and clean clothes, and calls me *Mary dear*, in a sort of slimy voice ... Of course, if I told the solicitor how she treats me most of the time, he'd take me away and probably send her to prison, but I don't dare tell him because he'd never believe me, and then I'd catch it, after he'd gone ...'

She began to feel sleepy in the sun and leaned back against the door post, watching the sea. It was so calm it looked thick and smooth, like syrup. Far out on the horizon, there was a slow steamer with gulls blowing in its wake like pieces of paper, and, nearer the shore, a smaller boat with a drowsily chugging motor, that was making for the beach.

Mary yawned. She was getting bored. It was always easy to begin a story, but hard to go on with no one to tell it to.

'I wish something really interesting would happen,' she said aloud, and then thought that perhaps if she closed her eyes and counted a hundred, something would.

She closed her eyes and counted slowly, but when she got to a hundred and opened them, nothing had changed except that the steamer was further away and the small boat nearer. There were four people in it, three men and a boy. The motor had cut out and the boat was close enough for her to hear the men's voices, though not what they said.

She watched them idly. One of her grandfather's walking sticks was leaning against the wall of the hut; she reached for it and began to poke at the shingle, still watching the boat which was gliding in over the silky water with hardly a ripple. Two of the men were dark-skinned and the third was white: a boatman wearing a beret. He was saying something; when he stopped, the others began to talk excitedly and wave their arms about, as if they were quarrelling.

They landed some way along the beach from Mary, and she stood up to watch. The bottom of the boat ground on the shingle and the two dark men jumped out, their trousers rolled up. The boatman handed the boy to one of them and pushed the boat out again. As soon as he was in deep enough water, he started the engine and made for the open sea.

The men on the beach stood, watching him go. They were oddly dressed for a sea trip; in dark suits, each carrying a small suitcase. Mary thought they looked lost and strange, because of their clothes and the way they looked about them once the boat had gone, as if they didn't quite know where they were.

Like castaways, Mary thought.

The boy sat down. He looked as if he were putting his shoes on. One of the men jerked him roughly to his feet and the boy flinched away, holding his crooked arm in front of his face.

The men began to run along the beach in Mary's direction. She shrank back, out of their sight, in the gap between her grandfather's hut and the neighbouring one.

They passed so close she could hear them breathing. They were running barefoot, stumbling on the stones. Once they were past, Mary waited a minute; then she peeped out, and saw the boy. He was following the men, but slowly; he was crying a little in a damp, dreary way, and he looked so *silly*, running along the beach in the bright sunshine, dressed up as if he were going to a party in a dark, long-trousered suit and a white shirt and a red bow tie, that quite without thinking, she stuck out her head and said *Boo* . . .

He was almost level with her. When she said *Boo* he gasped and turned with a look of such absolute terror that she was frightened herself and cringed back. Then he fell, all waving arms and thin legs, like a spider, banging his head on the hut steps.

And lay still.

Mary held her breath. For a moment she stayed as still as the boy on the ground. Then she came out of her hiding place between the huts and looked along the beach. The men had vanished. The only living things in sight were the gulls, resting on the calm sea like toys.

She looked down at the boy. He was lying on his face and her grandfather's walking stick stuck out from beneath him. She had left it leaning against the steps and he must have

THE BOY FROM THE SEA

tripped over it. Mary pulled at it gently but she couldn't move it. She was afraid of hurting him.

She said softly, 'Get up, you're not hurt,' but she knew, even as she spoke, that he couldn't hear her.

She said, 'Oh, *please* . . .' with a sob in her voice but only a gull answered her, swooping over her head with a long, sad cry.

Mary ran through the huts and on to the promenade. There were people about now, but they were some way away, by the pier. She went down the next flight of steps where there was a woman sitting in a deck chair, hidden from sight until now by a high breakwater. Mary started towards her but stopped almost at once. The old woman was lying back with her eyes closed, her shabby fur wrapped round her. It was the woman she had pulled the mad face at, this morning . . .

She couldn't wake *her*. And ask her to help . . .

Whimpering in her throat, Mary went back to the hut. The boy hadn't moved. A little wind had got up—no more than a gentle breath—and was stirring his limp, dark hair. His hands lay palm down on the shingles, the thin fingers loosely curled. One foot seemed to stick out at an awkward angle, and the side of his head was jammed up against the bottom step of the hut.

Mary knelt beside him. She thought she ought to turn him over and make him more comfortable, but she was afraid to touch him.

She thought—Perhaps he's dead! And then—*If* he's dead, I killed him!

She began to shake, crouching on the pebbles with her arms hugged round her. She looked up and down the beach. No one had seen her; if she locked the hut and went away, no one would ever know. She could go home for tea and say—

if anyone asked her—that she had been playing at the other end of the town, where the shell beach was. Aunt Alice and Grandfather would believe her. Whatever lies she told, they always believed her.

But this was one lie she couldn't tell! Suppose, after all, he wasn't dead? She couldn't just leave him here! She gave a little groan and put her hand down to his face. His cheek was warm and his breath fluttered against her palm like a bird's wing.

She stood up. Her stomach felt hollow and her legs seemed to be moving independently, like someone else's legs. They carried her up the steps, on to the promenade and towards the pier.

Just before the pier, there was a small crowd of people. She thought perhaps there had been an accident: there was a policeman there, though he wasn't in the crowd but on the edge of it, standing and looking out to sea.

Mary began to run towards him but slowed down when she was a few yards away. She remembered, with awful guilt, the Crunchie Bars she had stolen. Perhaps the man at the kiosk had missed them and told this very policeman. Perhaps he was looking for her now—for a dirty-faced girl with long, black hair. Forgetting she had washed before lunch, Mary pulled out her handkerchief, spat on it, and scrubbed at her mouth. She hesitated, gulped, went closer to the policeman—and then stopped dead.

The crowd beyond him had thinned and she could see, at the centre of it, the two men who had been in the boat with the boy. Another policeman was talking to them and a third was holding their arms just above the elbow, which was rather silly, Mary thought, because neither of them looked as if they would run away. They seemed far too sad and bewildered, and so out of place, somehow, standing on the sea front in dark suits, with small, shabby suitcases in their hands. Someone near Mary said, 'Poor devils . . .' and she looked up at the faces round her, but no one else seemed sorry: they were just staring and staring as if they were expecting—or hoping—that something exciting would happen.

But nothing did. There was a police car at the kerb, and as Mary pushed her way through the crowd, the two men and one of the policemen got into it, and drove away.

Mary wondered what they had done wrong. They had come from the sea, so perhaps they were smugglers, smuggling gold watches or diamonds. Or burglars—perhaps the boat that had landed them would call for them on the next tide to take them and their loot right away, where the police couldn't catch them. If they were burglars, it would explain why they had brought a boy with them. She remembered Oliver Twist, and how Bill Sykes had taken him burgling because he needed a boy small enough to get through a window and open the door from inside.

If the boy was a burglar, it was no good asking a policeman to help him. Or any grown-up, for that matter . . .

Mary had a sudden, awful feeling that everyone was watching her. She ducked her head, turned, and cannoned straight into the cushiony stomach of a large lady in a flowered dress. Her husband said, 'Watch out, can't you?'

Mary was going to say she was sorry, but then she saw Simon beyond them, on the other side of the road. He must have been standing there all the time, watching like the others, and now he was walking away.

Mary dodged round the large lady and flew across the road, looking neither to left nor to right—Aunt Alice would have had a fit if she'd seen her—and called, 'Simon, Simon, wait for me.'

She had forgotten he was bossy and inquisitive. She thought, a long time afterwards, that she must have known Simon would be a good person in an emergency, but in fact she couldn't possibly have known it then. She just acted without thinking, and when he stopped and she saw there was someone with him, she came to a halt and couldn't think what to say.

'Hallo,' Simon said. He looked shy for a minute, and then he said, 'This is my Gran. Gran—this is my friend, Mary.'

'Hallo, Mary.' Simon's Gran had a thin, merry face with a long, pointed nose, rather like a cheerful witch. She was pushing a pram with a baby in it. Mary thought it was the fat one she had seen in the play pen.

'That's Jane,' Simon said. 'And our new baby's called Jenny.' Jane blew a large bubble and laughed when it burst.

'Four sisters,' Simon's Gran said. 'Poor, down-trodden boy. Still, I suppose he'll live.'

Simon looked at Mary. 'Were you coming to see us? You came earlier, then you went away.'

So he *had* been watching from a window! For a second, Mary felt horribly embarrassed, then it didn't seem to matter. All that mattered was to get Simon alone, to tell him about the boy. She had the feeling—and it was growing stronger and stronger—that he would know what to do.

But how to get him alone? His Gran was smiling and saying, 'Well, why don't you come and see us now?' and she set off at a good, smart pace, without giving Mary a chance to answer. She couldn't even drop back and catch Simon's eye, because his Gran was talking to her, telling her that the new baby weighed eight and a half pounds, which was two pounds more than Jane had weighed when she was born and three pounds more than Polly-Anna, who were naturally smaller, being twins, but Simon had weighed more than any of them: nine pounds, three ounces exactly. '*And* his Mum only a little thing, knee-high to a grasshopper!' she said proudly.

Mary tried to think of a polite remark on this subject, but failed. All she could think of was to ask Simon's grandmother how much *she* had weighed when she was born, but that didn't seem the right sort of question, somehow.

'You sound like a cannibal, Gran,' Simon said. 'Working out which of us would have given you the biggest dinner!'

'Horrible boy,' his grandmother said calmly. She turned the pram into the front garden of Harbour View and began to unfasten the baby's harness. 'Come along my duckie-doo. Tea time now.'

'Roast baby with mint sauce,' Simon grinned at Mary. 'Are you coming? Tea time with the Trumpets is a *very* special occasion.'

Mary giggled. Then she shook her head. 'I can't, just now. There's something I've got to do . . .'

She looked helplessly at Simon who was capering round the pram, rolling his eyes and smacking his lips. 'Something awfully special . . .' she said, speaking loudly and willing him to stop acting the fool and pay attention . . .

But he barely glanced in her direction. He was too full of himself and his silly joke. 'We don't say *what's* cooking in our house, we say *who's* cooking,' he said, bounding up the steps in front of his grandmother and flinging the door wide. She pretended to box his ears as she passed and he doubled up, laughing. He shouted, to Mary, 'Of course, you can always have a peanut butter sandwich, if you don't fancy what's on the menu!'

Mary clenched her teeth. It was no use. When people were in this sort of mood, you could never get them to listen.

'I suppose you think you're witty,' she said. 'Mister Too-clever-by-half!'

She stumbled out of the gate her eyes scalding with disappointment. It had been a mistake to think Simon would help. He was too stupid, too cockily pleased with himself and his beastly family to bother about anyone else. She had been wasting her time.

And not only her time, she suddenly realised. The boy's time, too! While she had been chasing around, silly enough to believe she could find someone to help her, he might have been dying! She should never have left him alone, not without looking to see where he was hurt. Suppose he had cut himself when he fell, and was bleeding to death!

Fear grew as she ran. By the time she reached the bathing hut, she was so panic-stricken that she could hardly believe what she saw. Or, rather, what she didn't see . . .

The hut was as she had left it: the door standing open and the sun streaming in. But the boy had gone.

FOUR

'Anything might have happened to him . . .'

'I WAS ONLY trying to make you *laugh*,' Simon said. He sounded reproachful and slightly out of breath. When Mary didn't answer, he sat down beside her on the hut steps and pretended to be more puffed than he actually was, blowing out his lips and fanning himself. 'You run pretty fast for a girl,' he said.

Mary gave him a withering look and stuck her nose in the air.

Simon said, 'I know it wasn't a very good joke, about eating people, I mean. But it wasn't so terribly *bad*, either. Not bad enough to make you run away. Unless you believed it, of course . . .'

Mary knew he was expecting her to laugh. But she couldn't. She couldn't even smile. She just sat, hunched up and staring at the sea. Perhaps the boatman had seen what happened and come back and fetched the boy? But if he had done, wouldn't the boat be still in sight? She stared until her eyeballs ached. The sea was as empty as the sky.

'*Did* you believe it?' Simon was peering at her, leaning so close that she had to look at him. His face was wide open with laughter and his eyes seemed to reflect the speckles of light from the sea. 'You didn't really think we'd eat *you*?'

'Don't be *potty*.' Mary's voice was so frantic, he stopped smiling at once.

'Why did you run away, then?' He sounded surprised: he was the sort of boy, Mary thought, who would always expect an immediate and reasonable answer to everything. But she couldn't give him one, not now the boy had disappeared, because he wouldn't believe her. People *never* believed her, she thought miserably, and of course, quite often they were right not to, since she was always making up stories. Sometimes people said, 'Don't tell lies, Mary,' and sometimes, when they were kinder, 'Oh Mary, you have such an imagination!' As if imagination were a disease, like chicken pox, or measles.

Mary thought she wouldn't be able to bear it, if Simon said something like that. She clenched her fists and held her breath, almost as if she expected him to.

But all he said was, 'I'm sorry. I suppose it was the twins, then. I thought it might be. But you shouldn't have worried, honestly. I know they're awful, but they're not *sneaky*. Least, not when they understand. They wouldn't have *said* anything . . .' Mary stared at him and he blushed and added, lamely, 'About this morning, I mean . . .'

This morning seemed a long way away and a long time ago, like a dream she had almost forgotten. Remembering it now, Mary hung her head. 'It wasn't *that*, stupid.'

'What was it, then?' Simon's voice was still patient, but Mary thought she could detect a sharper note, as if in a minute or two he would begin to get bored with this one-sided conversation.

She looked at him quickly, prepared to be angry, but he only looked puzzled and interested and kind. Suddenly, she wished she could tell him. 'You wouldn't believe me if I told you,' she said, and stood up because she couldn't bear to sit still any longer. As she stumbled down to the creaming edge of the sea, her heart was beating fast and the palms of her hands felt sticky. Perhaps a policeman had found the boy! Perhaps he was even now shut up in jail, in a dark, airless cell! Or worse, dying in hospital with a doctor standing beside him and shaking his head and saying, *Of course, if we had found him earlier, we might have saved his life . . .*

'How d'you know I wouldn't believe you?' Simon said, behind her, and all at once the guilty fears that were simmering inside her seemed to bubble up and spill over. She turned on him furiously.

'Oh do shut up talking—talking's no *good*—we've got to *do* something quick.' Hot tears came into her eyes and blurred her vision. 'It's awful,' she said, half-sobbing, 'anything might have happened to him . . .'

'Who's him?' Simon said, and when she didn't answer—she tried to, but her throat seemed to have swollen up—he took her by the shoulders and shook her, quite hard. Then he let her go and said, 'Come on, tell me! Who's "him", and what's up?'

He had spoken in a jollying uncle-ish voice, as if Mary wasn't a girl his own age, but someone much younger—Poll, say, or Annabel. Another time Mary might have resented this, but now it comforted her. His sounding so calm and grown-up brought back the feeling she had had earlier; that here was someone who would know what to do.

Once she had begun to tell him, she couldn't get it out fast enough. 'You know those two men the policeman took away —well, there was a boy, too—he was running on the beach and—and I jumped at him and he fell over Grampy's stick. Then he didn't move and I thought—I thought he was dead— and I went to find someone and I saw the men with the police-man and I couldn't tell them because of Bill Sykes and Oliver

Twist and—and then I wanted to tell you, but you wouldn't listen—you just acted silly so—so I ran back and—and he's not here anymore . . . He's *gone* . . .'

She was out of breath and her legs felt funny, so she sat down on the breakwater.

Simon said slowly, 'Well, he can't be dead then, can he? I mean, corpses can't walk!'

Having made this practical point, he stopped and looked at Mary, frowning a little. Then he said, 'But I don't see—I mean, what you said about Bill Sykes and Oliver Twist. I don't see what that's got to do with it.'

Mary smiled. She was beginning to feel ashamed of her babyish behaviour—almost crying and being unable to get her story out sensibly—and was glad to find something Simon didn't know. She said, 'Bill Sykes was a burglar and he always took a boy with him when he went burgling to get through the windows he was too fat for and open doors for him. Haven't you read *Oliver Twist*?'

Simon nodded, but he still looked puzzled. He said, 'Don't *you* read the newspapers?'

This question didn't make much sense to Mary—unless Simon was just trying to get his own back! But she was going to answer it, all the same, and say that she didn't read them very often because her grandfather only took the *Financial Times* and that was a dull newspaper without any pictures, when she remembered that her grandfather was supposed to be blind and weak in the head as well! Things had been happening so fast that she couldn't remember for the moment whether this was something she had actually told Simon, or something she had been going to tell him, so she shook her head and said, 'I'm not allowed. My Aunt doesn't allow me.'

Simon opened his mouth and shut it again. Then he said,

'Oh. Well, it doesn't matter. We'd better *find* him—that's the first thing. If he's hurt, he can't have gone far.'

'I looked in our hut,' Mary said. 'Only in ours, but the others are mostly shut up.' Simon began to walk purposefully up the beach and she ran after him. 'There wasn't anyone else near, except the old lady, and she was asleep. And I couldn't have told the policeman, could I?' Simon had stopped by the hut. He didn't seem to be listening, so she plucked at his sleeve. 'After all, if he's a burglar, they'd have locked him up too!'

Simon looked at her. He was grinning. 'So that's what you thought, is it?' he said. And then, 'You silly nit.'

Mary said indignantly, 'What d'you mean?' but he shook his head at her and put his finger to his lips.

She said, 'Silly nit yourself,' but softly, under her breath, because the grin had gone from his face now and he was holding his breath, as if breathing distracted him.

They both stood quiet. At first Mary could hear nothing, except the sea sucking at the shingle. Then she heard something else. A tiny, scrabbling sound ...

Simon whispered, 'Did you look *underneath* the hut?'

And underneath was where they found him, scrooged up in a tight ball and as far away from the hut steps as he could get. He made no sound or movement as they crawled towards him, just stayed still, with his knees drawn up to his chest and the whites of his eyes showing, but when they were close enough he gave a choky gasp and hit out. His fists were hard as little rocks.

They slithered backwards, on their stomachs, out of range.

'Well, he's not hurt as bad as all that,' Simon said, rubbing the side of his head where a glancing blow had caught him. 'I suppose he must've knocked himself out when he fell, and then come round and crawled in here . . .'

'His foot's hurt,' Mary said. 'It looked twisted round.' She looked at the boy and said, loudly and clearly, as if, being foreign, he must also be deaf, 'Does your foot hurt?'

The boy stared. He was shivering all over like a wet dog. His eyes were enormous and the colour of plums.

'I don't suppose he speaks English,' Simon said.

'Do you speak English?' Mary asked, but the boy didn't answer. Only his eyes showed that he had heard her speak: they moved from Simon's face to hers. He looked very small and harmless now, but he reminded Mary of her cat, Noakes, when he had been given to her as a kitten. He had looked gentle and quiet enough, but as soon as anyone touched him, he had turned into a spitting bundle of fur and rage.

'We better think what to do,' Simon said.

Being bigger than Mary, he was more uncomfortable under the hut: to get out, he had to wriggle backwards, pushing with his elbows. Mary stayed behind and said to the boy, speaking quietly so that Simon shouldn't hear and laugh at her, 'I didn't mean to hurt you. Or frighten you, even. I was just being silly.'

He had stopped shivering, almost as if he understood. She said hopefully, 'What's your name?' and then pointed to herself and said, 'I'm Mary,' but there was no response. He just watched her, and then began to cry silently. The tears that welled up in his plum-coloured eyes and slipped down the side of his nose, were shiny and solid-looking, like lumps of mercury. Almost as if someone had broken a thermometer, Mary thought.

Simon called her from outside. She said, to the boy, 'Don't cry. I'll come back. Don't be frightened. I'll come back.' She

knew now that Simon was right, and the boy couldn't understand what she was saying, so she spoke in a crooning sing-song,
trying to calm him with the sound of her voice, as if he were a
wild animal or a baby. 'I'll look after you,' she said, and wished
she could put her arms round him and hold him tight and
safe. He was so little, so thin . . .

Simon said, 'Mary . . .' and she crawled to the edge of the
hut and looked up.

'I got him an ice-lolly,' Simon said. 'I heard the van going
by.' Mary stared up at him, squinting because it was so bright,
after the darkness under the hut, and he held out the lolly.
'Just to show him we're friends,' he said.

The lolly was wrapped in paper. Mary wriggled back under
the hut and tossed it towards the boy. He watched her for a
minute, not crying now, and then one small, brown hand
crept across the stones. He unwrapped the lolly and took a
bite, his eyes still on her face. 'Go on,' Mary said. 'It's nice.'

He took another bite, and was immediately sick. Mary
crawled out from under the hut, holding her nose. 'He's been
sick. It's an awful smell.' She felt she might be sick herself.
'What are we going to do?'

'I've been thinking,' Simon said. He stopped. 'But I haven't
thought of anything yet.'

'We ought to clean him up,' Mary said. She fetched a bucket
from the hut and went down to the sea. The sun was low and
red in the sky now, and a chilly breeze whipped off the water.
She climbed back up the beach with a full pail and said,
'We've got to think of something soon. He'll catch cold if he
stays here all night.'

Simon bent down and called. 'Come on now, come on out.
We won't hurt you.'

'I don't suppose he'll come for you,' Mary said.

Simon stood up. 'Perhaps not. You try. He won't be so scared of you because you're a girl and smaller.'

'In a minute,' Mary said. 'First, we've got to make up our minds. I mean—what are we going to do?' She wondered if she could take the boy home with her and then dismissed the idea. Aunt Alice got into what Grandfather called a 'fine old state' if someone just came to tea. Mary said, 'Could you take him home with you? There's a lot of people in your house, one more wouldn't make much difference.'

'I can't. My Dad's a policeman.' Simon went red, as if this were an embarrassing thing to admit.

'What difference does that make? When I told you about the burglars, you said I was a silly nit.'

Simon went redder still. 'So you are. Or a plumb *ignorant* nit, anyway. He's breaking the law, all right, but he's not a burglar. He's an—an illegal immigrant.'

Mary stared. Simon said, 'Didn't you really know? Not even when I asked you if you read the newspapers?'

Mary shook her head. The truth was, she was usually so busy with her own thoughts and with what was happening to her, that what went on in the newspapers, or on television, seemed boring and far away, like grown-up conversation.

Simon sighed. 'I suppose you know what an immigrant *is*?'

'Someone from another country who comes here to live. That's not against the *law*!'

'Well. Sometimes. I mean, there's lots of people who want to come here, or go to America, because they can't get jobs in their own countries. But not everyone can come who wants to. There's what's called a quota—just so many foreigners let in every year. And sometimes people who can't get a place on the quota try and sneak in some other way. Like those two men. Quite a lot land here because it's near to France. They get to France and then they pay someone to bring them across the Channel.'

Mary said, 'But *he's* only a boy. He couldn't get a job!'

'Perhaps one of the men was his father or uncle or something.'

Mary wondered if this was true. It hadn't seemed like that. When they landed from the boat, the boy had seemed scared, as if the men were strangers. And they had run off without looking back and left him behind, alone ...

Simon said, 'They were Pakistanis, I expect. My father says most of the ones who land here come from Pakistan. Or India, sometimes.'

'What'll happen to them?'

Simon shrugged his shoulders. 'They'll put them in prison and then, if their papers aren't right, they'll send them back where they came from. It seems awful bad luck, when they've spent all their money to come here, but my father says it's the only thing. He says ...'

Mary said, 'I think it's a mean and horrible thing to do! I mean, if they can't get jobs in their own countries, they'll just *starve*, won't they?'

'My father says there's no point in being sentimental,' Simon said. 'It's just the law. People have to stick to the law.'

He sounded so calm. As if he didn't care at all. Mary looked at him—and felt her skin begin to crawl with panic. She had been wrong about Simon! He might know what to do, but not in the way she had meant. He wouldn't help her to hide the boy! His father was a policeman! He would go and tell his father, because it was the law, and they would take the boy away and put him in prison.

She said, 'You better go. Just forget about it and go.'

'What's up with you?' He looked dumbfounded.

'Just that I've changed my mind. I'll look after him. You don't have to help. I don't want you to.'

'But what'll you do?'

'Mind your own business.' Mary stamped her foot. She could feel a fine, healthy rage burning up inside her. 'It's better you don't know, isn't it? After all, it might be against your precious, rotten law, mightn't it? I might be doing something *wrong!* And you're such an awful prig, you wouldn't really want to know!'

There was a twitch at the corner of his mouth as if he were trying not to smile. He said, 'You know, you did *ask* me . . .'

'That was before I knew your father was a policeman!'

For some reason, this went home. He said, 'All right, then,' and turned on his heel. The back of his neck was bright red as he walked away.

Mary called after him, 'If you tell anyone, I'll *kill* you,' but he didn't turn round.

She waited until he had disappeared, then she bent down to peer under the hut and call to the boy. He wasn't at the back anymore, but near the steps. It startled her to find him so close: it was almost as if he had been listening. She said, 'Come on now, it's all right, he's gone.'

She put out her hand towards him and, rather to her surprise, he took it and let her help him up. Standing, he was almost as tall as she was, though thinner; his wrists and the bones of his face so small and delicate that she felt clumsy. She sat him on the steps and washed him with the sea water from the bucket and her handkerchief.

She said, 'I expect you're hungry. The first thing, I'll have to get you something to eat. Not much, because you've been sick, just a little something to settle you. I expect it was the boat made you sick; I once went in a boat to France and I was sick all the time. And sometimes I'm sick for no reason at all, just over-excitement, Aunt Alice says, and it's better up than down. You'll feel better when you've had a little sleep. You could have a little sleep in the hut, I could put towels on the floor to be comfy, and then I'll have to think what to do, because you don't want to go to prison and be sent back to Pakistan, do you? So you'll have to be good and stay quiet and not make any noise and try not to be scared ...'

She rang out her handkerchief in the pail. He looked cleaner now and he didn't smell so badly, but his shirt was wet and the evening wind was flattening it against his chest and making him shiver.

She said, 'You'd better get out of that shirt. Wearing wet clothes is asking for trouble. I could give you my jersey. It'll be big on you, but it'll keep you warm ...'

He was watching her steadily and she sighed. It was no good talking. He couldn't understand, and it didn't really help her, either: it just put off the awful moment when she would have to decide what to do.

She turned away from him to empty the bucket and to spread out her handkerchief to dry on the stones. The sun had gone now, leaving a pale, candle-yellow light, stretched out thin on the horizon. The rest of the sky had filled up with small, puffed clouds, so that it looked mottled, like marble. It must be nearly supper time, and she would be expected home. If she was only ten minutes late, Aunt Alice would worry, and if Aunt Alice was worried, she was quite capable of telephoning the police.

Mary caught her breath and turned back to the boy.

He had taken off his jacket and was unbuttoning his shirt.

For a second, the significance of this didn't reach her mind, which was busy with the problem of Aunt Alice and the police.

Then she said, thunder-struck, 'You *heard* me. All the *time*.'

He didn't answer. His small face was expressionless as he slipped off his shirt and held out his thin, shivery hand for her jersey. It wasn't until she had taken it off and given it to him and he had pulled it over his head, that he finally spoke.

He said, 'I am not from Pakistan.'

Mary looked at him with her mouth open.

He said, 'I am from Kenya. My name is Krishna Patel. And I am a British Subject.'

He stood up, wearing her jersey, and looking, not thin and frightened anymore, but rather angry and proud, and suddenly Mary began to get angry too. He was such a cheat! She thought of all the things she had said to him—silly, gentle, soothing things that she would never have dreamed of saying to anyone who could understand her—and felt cold and humiliated.

She said, 'I think you're rotten! That was a rotten, mean, sneaky thing to do!'

She took a threatening step towards him, but he didn't back away, just stood quite still, his eyes widening with surprise.

She said, 'What did you do it for? *Pretending* . . .' but there was no time for him to answer her, because at that moment Simon appeared, bursting on them suddenly from the space between the huts. He was panting for breath and so pale that the freckles stood out on his face like stones.

'They're coming,' he gasped. 'They're coming along the beach . . .'

And when Mary and the boy stood motionless, he took the boy by the shoulders and pushed him into the hut. 'Get in,' he said. 'Behind the door. *Hide* . . .'

FIVE

Against the Law . . .

SO WHEN THE policemen came, trudging along the beach, all they saw were two children, sitting on the steps of an open hut and sorting out a pile of pretty shells.

They looked innocent enough. The only odd thing, perhaps, was that they didn't look up, even when the two men stopped in front of them.

'Bit old for shells, aren't you, Simon?' one of them said. His voice was friendly but his eyes were sharp. He looked, over the children's heads, into the hut.

Mary saw Simon's hand tighten on his knee, and knew he was going to blush. She tried to stop him, concentrating hard and saying, in her mind, *Don't blush, don't blush*, but it was no use. The colour swept up his neck, over his face, and disappeared into his hair. He said, 'Oh, Mr Peters! I didn't see you! This is my friend, Mary. I'm just helping her with her shells.

It sounded so false that Mary despaired. She said, 'It's for a Project at school. Life on the Seashore. I have to collect sea-weed and shells and things. It's frightfully boring, and I'm rather behind hand, that's why Simon's helping me.'

She spoke in a lively, natural tone, but without much hope. She was a better liar than Simon—who hadn't had much practice, by the sound of it—but she doubted if she had been convincing enough to distract attention from that blush. They would have to be imbeciles, or blind! Any minute now

one of them would push them aside and march into the hut,
and drag the boy from his hiding place behind the door.

She sat rigid, not daring to raise her eyes above the middle
button of Constable Peters' waistcoat, waiting for a heavy hand
on her shoulder and an angry voice, shouting.

What she heard, instead, was a chuckle. She looked up and
saw that both men were grinning broadly.

Constable Peters had a red, sweaty face, with small, brown
eyes sunk into it, like currants in a bun. He smiled at Mary.
'This your hut?'

'My grandfather's.'

'Lock it up when you go. Otherwise you might get un-
welcome visitors. You've not seen anyone, I suppose? No
suspicious characters hanging about?'

'Only you,' Mary said, which made them laugh. They
walked off, laughing and talking to each other.

When they were out of earshot, Simon said, 'I can't help it.
It's having a thin skin. The blood shows. And the more you
think about it and try and stop it, the worse it gets.'

Mary, who had been holding her breath, drew in a deep
gulp of air and felt dizzy. 'I thought they'd be bound to know.
Once you started. They couldn't not notice.'

'They noticed, all right. They just thought it was something
different, that's all."

'What?'

He gave her a shy look, picked up a small pink and brown
shell and began to examine it with great attention.

Mary jabbed her elbow into his arm and he dropped the
shell into the pile at his feet.

She said, '*What* did they think?'

He sighed. 'They thought it was because I was with you.
With a *girl*. Some people have queer ideas of what's funny.'

In the circumstances, Mary thought it was fairly funny herself.

'They'd laugh on the other side of their faces, if only they knew.'

She hoped this would cheer him up, but it didn't seem to. His expression remained glum.

She said, reproachfully, 'You wouldn't rather they'd guessed *right*, would you?'

He gave her a brief, scornful glance. 'I came back, didn't I?'

'Yes.' But this needed an explanation, she thought. She said, to his sullen profile, 'Why did you? I mean, after all you said about sending people back where they came from. It was the law, you said.'

He got up quickly, as if he didn't want to answer her question, and went into the hut. He said, 'Well, for crying out loud! His Nibs is asleep!'

The boy was curled up in the small space behind the door, his head dangling loose on his frail neck, like a heavy flower. He was snoring a little.

Simon said, rather uncomfortably, 'It's different with some-one you've *seen*.' He looked at her for a minute, and then began to grin. 'Besides, I suddenly thought what we could do with him!'

They sat on the steps. He couldn't stay here, Simon explained, because the police kept an eye on the huts. Tramps often broke in and slept in them.

'So I thought of my Uncle Horace's shop,' Simon said. 'He's not there and it's locked up, but I know a way in. We can take him after dark. After supper.'

'I have to go to bed after supper,' Mary said.

Simon looked amused. 'You can get out though, can't you? You'll have to come, you've made friends with him.'

'He speaks English,' Mary said. She had forgotten this. 'Just before you came back, he *talked* to me. And you were wrong about Pakistan! He comes from Africa—from Kenya. His name's Krishna Patel.'

From the hut behind came a small, creaky groan, as if Krishna had heard his name spoken in a dream. They went inside and he was stirring, rubbing his eyes.

'Shut the door,' Simon said, and Mary pulled it to, so that only a little light came in, through the cracks.

The boy lurched to his feet and tottered, moaning.

'Cramp,' Simon said. He rubbed the boy's legs with his knuckles. 'Stamp your feet. It'll bring the blood back.'

But the boy was too sleepy. He stood, swaying and yawning.

'Let him lie down,' Mary said. There were bathing towels on the hook: they smelt musty, but they were better than nothing. She spread them on the floor and put Krishna down. He curled up, thumb in mouth, like a baby.

'Out for the count,' Simon said. He knelt, and spoke in his ear. 'We're going to lock you in. But we're coming back. If you wake up, just *wait*. No noise!'

'You don't have to shout at him,' Mary said. She touched his cheek and he opened his eyes and looked at her. 'Why didn't you tell us you spoke English?'

He took his thumb out of his mouth. 'I was afraid,' he said.

Mary was a bit afraid, too. It was all very well for Simon to talk so calmly about getting out after dark: he didn't know Aunt Alice who prowled the house at night, bolting doors and windows against burglars, and who always came into Mary's room, last thing, to see she was safe in bed. It would be easier to escape an armed guard than Aunt Alice's vigilant eye! 'She's afraid I'll run away and tell someone about the way she

treats me,' Mary said, eating her supper by herself in front of
the television, because by the time she had got home, Grandfather and Aunt Alice had finished theirs, and Aunt Alice
had been putting on her coat to come and look for her.

Mary had explained that she had been playing with her new
friends and forgotten the time, and Aunt Alice had said, 'Don't
your friends have homes to go to?' She was only cross because
she had been worried, but remembering it now, Mary scowled
at the television and said to herself, 'She doesn't want me to
have friends because she's afraid I'll tell them about her.
She'd really like to keep me locked in my room, but she
doesn't dare, because the woman who comes in to clean might
think it funny . . .'

Coming in just then, Aunt Alice saw Mary's scowl and said
nervously, 'Finished, dear? Do you want anything else?'

Mary said nothing. She wished there *was* a lock on her door.
Then Aunt Alice couldn't come in . . .

'No answer came the stern reply,' Aunt Alice said brightly.
'Not an apple, dear? An apple a day keeps the doctor away.'

Mary's scowl grew fiercer. *Sneaking in after I'm asleep,* she
was thinking. *Like a thief, poking and prying.*

She said, 'Aunt Alice, I wish you wouldn't come into my
room, after I've gone to bed.'

Aunt Alice looked so hurt, that even Mary felt sorry.

She said, 'I only meant—it's sort of scarey, lying there and
knowing you're going to come, creeping in and looking at me
when I'm asleep.'

In the silence, Aunt Alice's stomach made a bubbling sound.
Then she said, 'I never meant to frighten you. Only to see
you're all right . . .' She looked at Mary quite sharply. 'I
didn't think you were a nervous little girl.'

'I'm not.' Mary tried to think how she would feel if she

were. 'It's just that things look different in the dark. Clothes on a chair and on the peg on the door. And if you're half asleep, and the door opens slowly, you're scared of what might come in . . .'

Aunt Alice smiled at Mary. 'Well, I won't, again. I used to be frightened of the dark, too. When I was a little girl, I had a nurse who used to lock me in the cupboard under the stairs when I was naughty. It was black as pitch.'

'Why did you let her? I'd have *screamed*,' Mary said.

Aunt Alice sighed. 'She said there was a crocodile there who would eat me up at one bite, if I made any noise.'

Mary thought it was typical of Aunt Alice to be so stupid. Perhaps what she was thinking showed on her face, because Aunt Alice said, 'Of course I knew there wasn't a crocodile. But only in the way *you* know the clothes on the back of the door are just clothes. That's why I always leave the light on the landing for you.'

Leaving the light on the landing seemed an odd jump from crocodiles in the cupboard, but it gave Mary something to think about. When she went to say goodnight a bit later on she kissed Aunt Alice as well as her grandfather. This was something she had avoided up to now, hating the idea of Aunt Alice's glasses and the stiff hairs on her chin. The cold rim of the glasses bumped her nose and the whiskers pricked her, but she minded less than she had expected and Aunt Alice seemed pleased: she gave one of her high-pitched laughs and said, 'Well, what an honour!'

Mary said, 'I think that was beastly, about the crocodile,' and backed away before Aunt Alice could kiss her again.

'Crocodile? What crocodile?' Grandfather said, but Aunt Alice only laughed again and said that was a secret, between her and Mary, and just look at the *time!* Didn't Grandfather want to watch that old war film on television? It was called *The Sinking of The Bismarck*, and he had definitely said, this morning, that he wanted to see it!

She sounded flustered. Of course, Mary thought, as she went upstairs, Aunt Alice would never have told Grandfather about the nurse and the crocodile, and she would be embarrassed if he found out now. She would be afraid he would blame himself for employing such a horrible woman to look after his daughter. At least, that was half of it. The other half was shame: she would hate him to know that something that had happened so long ago was still important to her.

Mary was surprised how sure she was about this. She didn't just understand how Aunt Alice felt, she *knew*. It was rather as if she had suddenly acquired a magic eye that could look into Aunt Alice's mind.

In much the same way—knowing, not guessing—she was sure that Aunt Alice would not look into her room again, not tonight nor any other night. Not because she had said she wouldn't, but because people creeping in was something she had been afraid of when she was a little girl.

Knowing this, Mary felt mean, but only for a minute. There was no more time to think about Aunt Alice. She had promised Simon to meet him at nine, and it was nearly that already.

She stood on the landing and listened. Stirring music rose up the stair well, followed by the sound of gunfire. Aunt Alice would not want to watch, Mary knew, she hated noisy war films, but she would sit with Grandfather all the same, in order to wake him when he dropped off to sleep because he hated to miss anything. And the film would last about an hour and a half ...

Mary crept down the stairs, out of the front door, and into the gusty dark.

Simon was waiting by the bathing hut. He said, 'I thought you weren't coming.'

'I had to wait till the film started. Have you got him?'

From the dark shadow between the huts, a darker shadow emerged. Mary giggled. 'He doesn't show up in the dark like you do.'

'The whites of his eyes show more, though,' Simon said.

Krishna was shivering. Mary took his hand and it felt cold and damp.

'If we run he'll get warm,' she said, but Simon shook his head.

'Just walk natural. It's better.'

It was more alarming, though. Once up on the promenade, they seemed so exposed. Naked, like shelled crabs. The line of houses facing the beach showed only an occasional light: anyone could be watching from a dark window. And side turnings could shelter policemen ... Mary longed to take to her heels and run, and she knew from the way Simon looked around him, that he was scared, too. Only Krishna seemed calm.

As they approached the pier, he said in a clear, penetrating voice, 'Is it far to London, from this town?'

'I don't know how many miles,' Mary whispered. 'It's about two hours on the train.'

'I should like to go to London now,' Krishna said. 'My Uncle is in London. He was to meet me at the airport.'

'Shut *up*,' Simon said. 'Look ...'

Just beyond the pier, a long, black car was parked at the side of the road.

'Police,' Simon said. 'No, don't stop. Keep walking.'

Mary felt as if her legs were bending under her. She clutched Krishna's hand.

Simon said suddenly and loudly, 'Do you know about the monk who was frying chipped potatoes?'

'No,' Mary said. She thought it seemed an odd time for jokes.

'Well. This other monk came up to him and said, are you a friar? And he said no, I'm a chipmunk.'

It was an old joke, and it hadn't been very funny when new. All the same, Mary laughed politely, and Simon laughed too. They were drawing level with the car, and Mary could see the nearest policeman's face, a pale blur turned towards them.

'Up here,' Simon said, and they turned up a side street. It was narrow and winding; as soon as they were round the first bend Simon said, '*Run* now,' and Mary and Krishna ran until he burst between them, breaking their clasped hands, and wheeled them into an alley.

The alley was full of dustbins. Mary stumbled against one, hurt her knee, and said crossly, 'What a time to make jokes!'

'I had to do *something*. There was that policeman, looking out of the car. So I told a joke, and all he saw was just three kids, telling jokes and laughing. It was a sort of camouflage.'

Mary rubbed her knee. Were they really looking for us?'

'Not for us, just for *someone*. My Dad was in, supper time, and he says they caught the boatman out in the Channel and found out he had three passengers. He didn't say anything about a boy, so they're looking for another man.'

Krishna said, 'Why did we run? My foot hurts . . .'

He was leaning against the wall by the dustbins, one leg drawn up, like a stork.

Mary said to Simon—accusingly, because she had forgotten about it herself—'I told you he hurt his foot when he fell.'

She knelt down and felt the boy's ankle. It was swollen; hard and smooth as an apple. 'It must have been agony to walk on, even,' she said. 'Why didn't you tell us?'

For answer, he gave a little sob and Simon said, encouragingly, 'It's not much further. Just over the wall, and then it's quite easy.'

They had to stand on a dustbin. Simon got up all right and sat straddled on the wall to help Krishna, but the first time Mary climbed on to the dustbin, the lid tipped and she landed inside. The bin was full of squashy rubbish that felt slimy against her ankles and smelt foul.

'My God, you do pong,' Simon said, when she managed the climb on the second attempt, and sat on the wall between them. 'Wish I'd remembered to bring my smelling salts,' he went on, fanning his hand and pretending to feel faint.

'Witty, aren't you!' Mary said sourly, but Krishna laughed. It was such an odd, shrill sound, that they did not realise what it was at first. Then they saw that he was convulsed with laughter, rocking backwards and forwards on the wall and cheeping thinly, like a baby bird.

Somewhere a sash window went up with a rattle, and Simon said, 'Ssh . . . get *down*.'

He dropped into the yard on the other side of the wall and put up his arms for Krishna. Mary heard him gasp as he took the boy's weight. Then she jumped down beside them, and felt her bones jar.

There were more dustbins. 'Your Uncle must have an awful lot of rubbish,' Mary said.

'That's his business,' Simon said, and giggled faintly. 'Watch out, there's steps here.'

The steps led down to a dark area where there was a door and a barred window. Simon felt the bars and seemed to shake them gently.

'Who d'you think you are? Tarzan?' Mary said.

'My secret is discovered,' Simon said. He gave a little grunt, and two bars were swinging free. He glanced at Mary, grinning; then reached through to ease the window up.

He climbed in first, then Krishna, then Mary. It was dark and smelt of mice. 'Where are you?' Mary said, and walked forward, hands outstretched. She touched Krishna's jacket which was dry now, but stiff with sea water; then Simon's arm.

He said, 'One thing—we won't lose you. We just have to follow our noses.'

'Oh stop it.' Mary's voice rose. 'It's simply not *funny*—not going on and on.'

There was a little silence. He said, 'Sorry. Bad habit.' But she heard him sigh in the darkness and guessed he was hurt. Perhaps he was shy, she thought suddenly: people who kept on making jokes often were.

She said, 'Can we put on a light?'

'The electricity's off. But I've got my torch.'

He snapped on a thin, pencil beam. Mary could see his eyes gleaming above it. Then he swung it round, and she gasped. Except for the space where they stood, the room was crowded with statues: naked girls, stone lions, and, in one corner, a huge, wooden figure of a woman, in brightly painted draperies. She was leaning forward, hands clasped across her breast, and her head was lifted, the painted eyes staring.

'Off an old sailing ship,' Simon said.

Perhaps it was a trick of the torchlight, or perhaps it was that the figure was cunningly carved, but as Mary looked, the waves of the gold hair seemed to ripple, as if blown backwards in a wind.

'I don't like it,' Krishna said. His cold hand crept into Mary's. 'I don't like it here.'

'You don't have to stay,' Simon said. 'Not in this room.'

He led them out, through a dark passage where the smell of mice was stronger still, into another room. Here there was a higgledy-piggledy collection of furniture: tables, chairs, chests of drawers, old stoves, tin baths full of china ornaments. Mary looked where Simon shone the torch and saw spotted dogs, jugs and teapots. All of them were old, and most of them were broken. 'Are they antiques?' she asked, awed.

Simon shook his head. 'There's some better stuff upstairs, in the shop, but it's mostly rubbish. Uncle Horace says people'll buy anything on holiday, especially when it rains.'

Krishna said, 'My father has a shop. But it is not like this. In my father's shop, all is new.'

Afterwards Mary realised how strange and terrifying it must have been for him, to come to England from Africa and find himself in a dark, locked-up shop full of old statues and broken china. But at the time, she thought he was simply being rude, suggesting that Simon's Uncle's shop was a horrid, rubbishy place.

'I think it's lovely,' she said. 'Much more interesting than an ordinary shop.'

But at the same time, she wondered who could possibly want to buy a teapot without a handle, or a saucepan with a hole in the bottom.

Krishna said, 'People must be very poor in England to want to buy these old things.' His voice trailed into a little sob. 'My Uncle is not poor. I want to go to London, to my Uncle.'

Simon said, 'You can't. Not tonight. You'll have to sleep here.' He took Krishna's hand. 'Over here . . .'

Tucked away behind a big wardrobe that jutted out into the room, was a Victorian couch, upholstered in faded red material.

'It's quite comfy, really,' Simon said, bouncing on it. Springs twanged and a cloud of dust rose.

'I would rather sleep in a bed,' Krishna said, ungratefully, Mary thought.

'Then want must be your master!' she said, which was something people had often said to her. 'You'll sleep where you're jolly well put. You're jolly lucky to have anywhere to sleep at all. If it wasn't for us, you'd be in a prison cell on bread and water.'

'Don't bully,' Simon said. 'I don't think he understands.' He put his arm round the boy's shoulder. 'Lie down now. I'll find something to cover you.'

Krishna lay down submissively. Simon shone the torch on a jumble of old clothes in a corner and pulled out a shawl. It was made of yellowing silk and embroidered with red and purple flowers. 'It's Chinese,' Simon said. 'A bit raggedy, but it feels nice.'

He spread the shawl over Krishna; over its fringed edge, the dark eyes looked up at him, lost and sad.

Simon said, 'We've got to go now. But we'll come back in the morning. There's a lavatory down the passage. I'll leave the torch. You won't be scared, will you?'

Krishna didn't reply but his fingers moved on the shawl, stroking and pleating it.

Simon touched Mary's elbow. 'Come on,' he said softly. 'He'll be all right now.'

So they left Krishna Patel to sleep his first night in England, on a Victorian couch, covered with an old, Chinese shawl.

They didn't speak until they had climbed the wall again and were out in the alley.

Then Simon said, 'It's a daft thing we've done, you know. You won't tell anyone, will you? Not a single word ...'

He sounded so urgent that Mary felt nervous. She said, 'All

we've done is to look after him and find him somewhere to sleep.'

'It's against the law, though,' Simon said gloomily. 'Assisting a criminal to avoid arrest. Maybe it's not as bad as that, but it's bad enough . . .'

'Bad enough for what?'

Simon looked at her in the light of a street lamp. 'Just bad enough,' was all he said, but his expression, solemn and brooding, made her spine shiver.

Kidnapped

'DO CHILDREN GET sent to prison, Grampy?' Mary asked at breakfast.

Last night, safely back in bed while Grandfather and Aunt Alice were still watching *The Sinking of The Bismarck*, she had decided that this was what Simon had meant. What they had done was bad enough to get sent to prison for. The idea did not disturb Mary, in fact, she thought it would be interesting and exciting to be arrested and sent to prison, but she could see that it might worry Simon. Since his father was a policeman, he was bound to be more concerned about breaking the law.

'Not prison, no. A special school, sometimes, if they've been very naughty. Why? What have you been up to?'

'Nothing. I just wondered.' Mary looked innocent—a shade too innocent, perhaps. Her grandfather put down his newspaper and looked at her over the top of his spectacles.

She said quickly, 'I'm making up a story about some children who help a criminal to avoid arrest. He's—he's a burglar, he's robbed a bank, and the children hide him from the police.'

'Compounding a felony, I see. Well, of course that's a serious matter.'

But Grandfather was smiling, picking up his paper again and pushing his spectacles up on his nose.

'I want to know what'll happen if they're found out,' Mary said.

'It would depend. On how old they were, what sort of homes they came from. Whether they knew what they were doing.'

'Oh, they know *that*. One's a girl about my age, and there's a boy, a bit older. The girl's a rich orphan. She lives with her wicked Uncle who looks after her because he wants her money. She knows he hates her, but she daren't tell anyone, because she's frightened.'

Mary had been going to say 'Aunt', but she thought 'Uncle' was more tactful.

Grandfather said, 'She wouldn't be sent to prison, Mary,' and glanced at Aunt Alice, across the table.

Aunt Alice dabbed her mouth with her napkin. 'It sounds a sad story, dear. Why don't you make one up about nice people, instead?'

'Nice people are boring.' Mary frowned, pretending to think, and went on, very casually, 'Perhaps it isn't a burglar they help, then. It could be an illegal immigrant—an Indian from Kenya, or someone like that.'

'That would be quite different from a burglar,' Aunt Alice said. She sounded indignant, and her neck reddened.

Grandfather looked amused. 'Your Aunt means that an illegal immigrant is not a criminal, Mary. And Indians from Kenya are rather a special kind of immigrant. Kenya used to belong to England . . .'

'I know *that*,' Mary said. She hated to be told things she already knew.

'Well, then. When Kenya became independent, the Indians who lived there were afraid they would be badly treated under an African government. So they were offered British Passports, just in case. And now things *have* gone wrong—they're not being ill-treated by the Africans, exactly, but things are being made difficult for them in the way of jobs, and schools for their children, and so on—a lot of them have decided to use their British Passports and come to live in England. But *our* government has just passed a new law saying they can't come, after all. At least, not of right. They've got to take their turn with all the other people who want to come here—wait in the queue, so to speak.'

'It's disgraceful,' Aunt Alice said. 'Going back on our word!'

'Well. Yes.' Grandfather looked at Mary. 'There is another side, of course.'

'I'm afraid I don't see it,' Aunt Alice said.

'I don't, either,' Mary said. 'I think it's just *rotten*, passing a law like that! Stopping people! I don't see why people shouldn't live where they want to live.'

'It's a point of view, certainly.' Grandfather was watching her thoughtfully and although Mary was sure she had said nothing to make him suspicious, she felt uneasy, suddenly. He was the sort of person who often seemed to listen not only to what you said, but to what you didn't say . . .

Now he was beginning to pull at the top of his ear and stroke the back with his thumb . . .

Mary said quickly, 'Aunt Alice, could I have some sand-wiches to take on the beach? I got awfully hungry yesterday.'

Aunt Alice looked startled at this sudden change of subject, but pleased. 'Of course, dear. As long as it won't spoil your lunch.'

'Not with all this good sea air. I get so hungry. Hungry as *a horse*.'

'Hunter, dear.' Aunt Alice beamed fondly. 'What kind of sandwiches? Would tomato be nice?'

'I don't suppose he likes tomatoes,' Simon said. 'He's fussy. I fried him an egg for breakfast and put it between two bits of bread and he looked at it as if it was a dead mouse, or something.'

'Cold fried egg sounds almost as nasty,' Mary said.

The chipped, gold lettering over the door of the shop said HORACE TRUMPET ANTIQUES AND BRIC À BRAC. Mary stared into the dusty window and two large, spotted china dogs seemed to stare back at her sadly.

'He might at least have said thank you,' Simon said. 'But he just looked at it and said *Is this all?* as if he was a prince or a maharajah or something. Then he said, *When will you take me to my Uncle?* As if I was a servant!'

He sounded very grumpy. Mary thought perhaps he was frightened. She said, 'We won't get sent to prison, you know.'

''Course not. Kids don't get sent to prison. It's just that I don't see what we're going to do! I mean, it was all very well, rescuing him last night, and it was fun in a way, but I've been thinking since. I didn't sleep a wink last night!' He glared at Mary as if this was her fault, then heaved a deep sigh and kicked moodily at a jutting paving stone. 'I suppose he can stay in the shop for a bit, till Uncle Horace comes back, but he can't stay there for ever.'

'I don't suppose he wants to! He's got this Uncle in London hasn't he? All we've got to do is ring up and say he's here. Then we can take him to the station and put him on a train and his Uncle can meet him. If he hasn't got any money for the fare, I've got some in my Pig.'

She thought it was a pity, really, that the solution was so simple; the adventure ending when it had only just begun.

'Oh, big deal!' Simon said. 'Why not ring up the police while you're about it? Do you think they're not watching the trains? They'll have someone at the station on the lookout for

suspicious characters, and he'll be caught, and *we'll* be in dead
trouble . . .'

'That's all you care about, isn't it?'

'No it isn't, if you want to know!' Simon went red as fire,
and Mary remembered how he had run back to warn them last
night, when he needn't have done . . .

She said, 'Well. Anyway, he's not a suspicious character. I
think you're just foul to say that!'

'Wait till you see him,' Simon said. 'His foot's swollen up
and he's got a great lump on his head. I suppose it didn't
notice last night in the dark, but it's big as an egg this morning.
He looks as if he's been in a fight.'

Mary said patiently, 'Well his Uncle'll have to come and
fetch him, then! We'll explain Krishna's hurt, and his Uncle'll
come and fetch him by car.'

'First catch Uncle,' Simon said.

'What on earth d'you mean?'

He shrugged his shoulders. 'If he *has* got an Uncle in England,
and he was supposed to meet him at the airport, why did he
turn up by boat?'

'It's no good asking me,' Mary said. 'I don't know, do I?'

'I was kidnapped,' Krishna said. He was sitting on the couch
with his bad foot propped up and the Chinese shawl round his
shoulders. He looked both exotic and sinister, with the shawl,
and his dark skin, and the huge lump on his forehead which had
half closed one eye. He would certainly be noticed if they took
him to the station—Mary had to admit Simon was right about
that, though he had been wrong about the tomato sandwiches,
which Krishna ate with relish while he talked.

'The plane was supposed to fly straight from Nairobi to
London but we landed in France because one of the engines

went wrong. We waited for a bit, and then we got on a train. There were hundreds of people—a lot of poor French people and peasants and women in black clothes—and we were all squashed in together. I went to sleep and when I woke up it was dark outside and I was hungry. A man in my carriage gave me some sweets and said, where was my mother and father? I said they had had to stay behind in Nairobi because my mother got sick, but they would come later on and buy a fine house in London and I would go to school. He said, did I really think they would let me into England, a boy on my own? I told him my Uncle would meet me, but he just laughed and asked if I had any money. He said, if I had, he knew a way to get into England without trouble. He didn't speak English very well. He was Indian like me, but not from Kenya, and he had very poor clothes. I thought he was probably a robber, so I pretended to go back to sleep and after a bit, he got up and went away.

'When we got to Paris, we got into a bus and went to the air terminal. Someone said there was a plane going to England, but there weren't enough seats on it. Everyone was pushing and shouting and some people were crying. Then the stewardess who had been on the plane came up to me and said it was too late to get to England now, and the best thing would be for me to go home to Kenya. She said she would put me on the next plane back, so when she went away, I ran and hid in the lavatory.

'What do you mean, too late to get to England now?' Simon said.

'Because of the new law, of course. Do you not know about the law? Our plane had to arrive in London before midnight, or they would not let us in.'

'Sounds pretty funny to me,' Simon said. 'Like Cinderella, or something.'

He began to laugh, but Mary stopped him. 'Do be quiet. I think I know what he means and I'll tell you later, but do be quiet now . . .' She turned to Krishna who had finished the last sandwich and was shaking the crumbs from the shawl. 'How long did you hide in the lavatory?'

'Quite a long time . . .' For a minute, he looked frail and scared, as if remembering how lonely he had been, hiding in a lavatory in a strange country in the middle of the night. Then he sat up straight and said, 'I was not afraid, of course. It was just that I did not know what to do. After a while I went out, into the hall. It was full of people, waiting, and I saw the man who had been on the train. He was sitting on one of the seats and I thought, perhaps he was not a robber after all. He saw me and smiled, so I went up and asked him how I could get a plane to England. He said the planes were full, but it would be easy if I had money for a bribe, and I told him that I had fifty pounds in English bank notes that my father had given me for my Uncle. He said he thought that would be enough, and if I would wait he would go and find out. He gave me his seat and I went to sleep and when I woke up the man had come back with another Indian and a Frenchman. The Frenchman looked rough, like a peasant. I started to take my money out of my pocket but he stopped me. I thought perhaps he was an airport official and he did not want to be seen taking a bribe, so I went out of the hall with the men, into the street. We got in a car and I showed my money and the Frenchman took it, and laughed. He started the car and I thought we were going to the airport, so I was happy and sat looking out. Paris is a very dirty city, not like Nairobi, and I was surprised at this, because I thought France was a rich country. We drove along, through some poor streets, and I said, *It is a long way to the airport*, and the Indian said we were not going to England on a plane, but by boat. Of course, I was very angry, but when I said so, they laughed at me, and then, when I told them to stop the car and let me get out, the man who was sitting in the back with me, twisted my arm behind my back until I thought it would break. It is still painful here . . .'

He touched the upper part of one arm with the other hand and a flicker of remembered fear crossed his face, so that Mary, who had been envying him this exciting adventure, felt a little frightened herself.

Krishna said, 'Of course, *then* I knew that these were not good men but wicked ruffians, and if I did not keep quiet, they would do me some terrible harm—slit my throat, perhaps, and leave me bleeding to death in the street! So I did not speak again and sat very still, for hours. I tried to think of some way to outwit them, but they were three desperate men against one boy! And although the two men went to sleep after a while, the Frenchman was watching me all the time in the driving mirror . . .'

Simon said abruptly, 'They couldn't have been *really* wicked. I mean, they did bring you here. They could just have stolen all your money and left you behind, in France.'

'They would not have dared do that!' Krishna's undamaged eye glistened. 'Because I would have told a policeman, and then they would never have escaped! He would have stopped them before they got to the boat!'

'Not if they'd murdered you, first! Dead men tell no tales!' Simon looked triumphant. 'You never thought they would, did you? You're just pretending!'

'Oh—don't be so *pernickety*.' Mary felt angry with him for butting in and spoiling a good story. 'Pernickety and *dull*,' she said, and glared.

Simon flushed pink, but he stuck to his guns. 'I just don't

see any point in exaggerating things! Saying they were desperate men!'

He looked miserable. For a moment, Mary was irritated—he was so stubborn, and, at the same time, so easily hurt—and then she felt sorry. He was right, after all. Those two men had looked anything but desperate—just dreadfully wretched and scared.

She said slowly, 'I don't suppose they'd have killed him. I expect they just wanted his money to help them get to England. But he must have been afraid they might, all the same. I know I would have been!'

'They were quite kind to me on the boat,' Krishna said. 'I had never been on the sea before and it was terrible—great waves and miles of cold, grey water, and no land! But the Frenchman gave me some brandy to stop me feeling sick, and the men said that when we got to England, they would take me to London, on a lorry, and I could find my Uncle. But when we landed, they ran away . . .'

'I expect they got frightened,' Mary said.

Krishna nodded. 'I was afraid too. It was not as I had expected. I thought there would be lots of tall buildings and soldiers in red jackets and fur hats. My Uncle had sent a picture postcard to show me.'

'Busbies,' Mary said. 'That's what the fur hats are called. But you only see dressed up soldiers like that in London. At Buckingham Palace where the Queen lives.'

She wondered what she would expect to find if she suddenly landed in Africa. Lions, she thought, and giraffes, and miles of desert, and naked black men waving spears.

She said, 'I don't suppose Africa's like what I think it is, either.'

'It is beautiful,' Krishna said. 'Where I live, it is beautiful.'

He smiled sadly at Mary and then looked at Simon, who was sitting on the end of the couch and staring impassively at the ground. Mary wondered if he was upset because she had called him dull and pernickety, or if he didn't believe Krishna's story. She wasn't sure that she believed it herself—it seemed too exciting to be altogether true—but she thought it was mean of Simon not to pretend to! 'I wish I hadn't left,' Krishna said, and his voice shook. 'I wish I hadn't come.'

Simon looked up. 'Well you have, haven't you? So there's no point in crying over spilt milk. What we got to do is to think what to do *now*.'

'*You* have to do nothing!' Krishna swung his legs off the couch and stood up, stiff and proud, although his lips were quivering. 'My Uncle Patel is rich! He will come and fetch me in his Cadillac! There is no need for you to help me, if you don't want to!'

He stamped his foot, gave a little moan, and staggered. He would have fallen if Simon had not jumped up to catch him, and sit him down again, on the sofa.

'My foot hurts . . .' Krishna said, with a sob, and although this was certainly true, Mary guessed that he had only said it to cover up the fact that he had been hurt in quite a different way.

A little to her surprise, Simon seemed to understand this too.

He said, 'Of course I want to help, softie! That's what I've been thinking about! What's the best thing to do. I mean, we don't want to do the *wrong* thing. Not just for you, though that's most important, but for us, too. If you get caught for being an illegal immigrant, then we'll get into trouble for hiding you, specially me. I mean it's Uncle Horace's shop, and Uncle Horace is my Dad's brother, and my Dad's a policeman

—it would look awfully bad for *him*. They mightn't believe he didn't know.'

Mary saw this was true. Simon had more to worry about than she had. It explained a lot—all his grumpiness and gloom.

Not that he seemed gloomy now. Perhaps sitting and thinking had done him good, because his voice sounded cheerful and confident.

'You can't go chasing up to London on your own because the police might catch you. But we can telephone this Uncle of yours and tell him you're here. I expect he'll know what to do.'

He said this as if he had thought of it for himself. Just as if it hadn't been Mary's idea in the first place! She felt indignant for a minute; then she saw the funny side, and smiled to herself.

Krishna smiled too. 'I do not have his telephone number but I remember his address. It is near Buckingham Palace. The street is called Buckingham Palace Terrace and his house is Number Four.'

Simon was looking at him rather oddly, Mary thought. 'Are you sure?'

Krishna's smile faltered. 'I think so. It was written down in a little book in my suitcase. But I left that behind in France.'

'Oh,' Simon said. 'Hmm.'

'We could write a letter,' Mary said.

Simon shook his head. 'A letter's dangerous. It might fall into the wrong hands. Specially if...' He stopped and blushed.

Mary said, 'We can look up the telephone number. We've got the address, and the name.'

'I suppose so,' Simon said. He was looking depressed again, and he sighed before he went on. 'There'll be telephone directories up in the shop. You go and get the right one, and

I'll see to his ankle. I took a bandage out of our medicine chest. If I wind it round good and tight, it won't hurt so much when he stands on it.'

'I wish you would not speak about me as if I was not here,' Krishna said. He lay back on the sofa and extended his foot. 'But you may bandage it if you wish,' he went on, speaking graciously and kindly as if he were a little king, and Simon one of his courtiers. Of course he couldn't really be a king, Mary thought—rather reluctantly, because it would have made a marvellous story if he had been! Much more likely that he was a spoiled, if good-mannered only child.

'Have you got any brothers or sisters?' she asked, and they both turned to look at her with such surprise that she giggled inside.

'No brothers. I have five sisters, but it is sad for my father to have only one son,' Krishna said. 'Why do you want to know?'

'No reason. I was only asking,' Mary said.

Five sisters, she thought, as she climbed the stairs from the basement. That would explain the lordly air! In India, girls waited on men. Krishna's sisters probably waited on him hand and foot!

Simon's voice floated up behind her. 'The desk's in the corner. Far side of the window.

But she didn't see the desk at once. The shop was dim and full of dust—not only on the furniture, but floating in the shafts of sunlight through the grubby window. And there were so many other things to see—Mary thought she had never seen so many interesting things in one room in her life. An old musical box with little drums inside that began to rattle and beat when she lifted the lid; a clock built into the middle of a wonderfully coloured china castle with turrets and battlements; a miniature rocking horse with a tiny, scarlet saddle, and what felt like real hair for its curling mane; a big, old harp that made a bubbly sound, like music under water, when she ran her fingers along the strings.

The desk was behind the harp and had been half-hidden by it; an ordinary desk covered with papers, some of them held down by a glass paper weight that had a strange, purple flower in the centre. She picked up the weight and it felt heavy and cool in her cupped hands. She looked into it, turned it, and the purple flower changed shape, swelled, or grew small. She held it up to the light so that she could see her hand, holding it; through the rounded top it looked huge, and she could see the lines on her fingers.

She had quite forgotten she could be seen from the street, and when someone tapped on the window, she almost dropped the weight. For a second, this was all that concerned her—she might have broken this beautiful thing, and nothing and nobody could have mended it. But as she put it back, safe on the desk, a different fear struck her.

Someone was outside the shop, watching her. And she had no business here . . .

SEVEN

Roast Pork and Apple Pie

AT FIRST, SHE dared not turn her head, or could not, rather—
she stood, staring at the paper weight, as if she had been turned
to stone.

Then a small voice shouted, 'Stand on your liver or die!' and
the spell was broken. She looked and saw the twins, Poll and
Annabel, their noses pressed into flat, white blobs against the
window.

She flew to the door. There was a bolt high up. The twins
watched her, giggling and nudging each other, while she stood
on a chair to reach it.

'What are you doing?' Annabel said, as soon as she had let
them in.

'Stealing again,' Poll nodded solemnly. 'She's a stealer.'

'Stealing's wrong, isn't it, Poll?'

'We stopped her, though.'

'She's a poor orphan girl,' Anna said sorrowfully. 'No one's
ever told her what's wrong and what isn't.'

Mary drew a long breath and hissed it out slowly. This must
be what Simon had told them. It was humiliating.

Poll smiled kindly. 'It's all right, poor Orphan Mary. Don't
be scared. We won't tell.'

'I wasn't stealing.'

Mary spoke so fiercely that they backed away, their round
eyes suddenly timid. She went on, more gently, 'I know it looks

funny, me being here, but it's all right. Simon wanted to show me some of your Uncle's things. The harp and the musical box ...'

She daren't go down to fetch him, in case they followed her. She stood at the top of the stairs and shouted, 'Simon. *Simon.* Polly-Anna's here.'

'What?' He came along the passage and looked up at her. 'What did you say?'

'Poll and Anna are here,' she repeated helplessly, hoping he had closed the door of the basement room and that Krishna wouldn't take it into his head to follow him.

Simon ran up the stairs. 'Why didn't you tell me, 'stead of just shouting?' he said unfairly. He pushed past Mary and shoo-ed the little girls back into the shop.

'What did you come for? You know you're not allowed. You touch things ...'

'*She* let us in,' Poll said. 'An' *she* was touching.'

'Picking things up.'

'*Looking* at them.'

'They thought I was burgling,' Mary said.

Simon looked at her, as if wondering, for a minute, if she had been. She met his gaze steadily and he blushed and said, 'Sorry!'

'Sorry for what?' Anna said.

'Nothing.'

'But you must be sorry for *something*.' Anna stood between them and looked, first into Mary's face, then into Simon's. 'You didn't tread on her, or anything?'

'No.' Simon grinned at Mary shyly.

She grinned back, and Anna had to pull at her sleeve to get her attention. 'Do *you* know why he said sorry?'

'Yes.'

'Why?'

'It was just something he thought for a minute.'

'Did he tell you?'

'No. I guessed.'

'What did you guess?'

'That's a secret.'

'I like secrets.' Anna slid her warm, rough hand into Mary's and squeezed it tight.

'So do I,' Poll said.

'Well, we'll have a secret sometime, just you and me,' Mary said, smiling at Simon and thinking, suddenly, how nice it would be to have two funny little sisters to tease and have secrets with. And to tell stories to . . .

'Tell us a secret now,' Anna said. 'Please, Mary.'

She caught Simon's eye. He nodded at her, and while she settled in a chair, the twins pressing against her knees, he took a telephone directory from the desk and went quietly downstairs.

'I'll tell you a story that's a sort of secret, if you like,' Mary said.

'We don't like stories about fairies,' Poll said. 'Only about people.'

'All right,' Mary said. 'Once upon a time, there was an orphan girl. Her mother and father had died in a terrible plane crash—there was nothing left of them except their teeth and a few burned bones—and she had to go and live with her blind old grandfather and her cruel Aunt . . .'

'Was she *strict*?'

'Oh, much worse than strict! Really wicked. She knocked her about and only gave her scraps and things to eat . . .'

Mary sank her voice to a thrilling whisper and told them about the blue bottle marked Poison, and how the wicked

Aunt stole into the orphan's room to look at her when she thought she was asleep, and watched her when she was ill, hoping she'd die, and wouldn't let her make friends with anyone, and took her toys away . . .

The twins listened, solemn-eyed and breathing heavily.

'Does she kill her in the end?' Poll asked suddenly. 'I mean, does the girl kill the Auntie?'

'I would if I was her,' Anna said. 'I'd shoot her—bang, shee-ow!'

'Bloodthirsty!' Simon said, from the back of the shop.

'Well. No. I don't think so.' Mary hoped Simon hadn't been listening long. 'I think what happens is, she runs away in the end, right away where no one can get her. A desert island, or somewhere good and safe, like that.'

'Are you going to run away, Orphan Mary?' Poll said.

'The only person who's going to run anywhere is you,' Simon said. 'D'you know the time? Nearly twelve, and Mum'll be expecting us home for Sunday dinner.' He looked at Mary. 'Would you like to come too? I mean, if you're hungry . . .'

Since she had told him Aunt Alice didn't give her enough to eat, she could hardly say 'no', straight out.

She said, 'I've got to be back, about half-past one.'

'That's all right,' Simon said. 'We eat early, Sundays.'

'Trouble is, people are always making up stories,' Simon said, when they were walking along the front and the twins were running ahead, out of earshot.

Mary felt uneasy, but only for a second. He wasn't talking about her, but about Krishna. There were a great many Patels in the London telephone directory, but not one in Buckingham Palace Terrace.

'That doesn't mean his Uncle doesn't live there,' Mary said. 'He may just not be in the telephone book.'

'It was an old one,' Simon admitted. Then he sighed. 'But Buckingham Palace Terrace is in Belgravia, where all the Embassies are. You'd have to be pretty rich to live there.'

'Krishna says his Uncle is.'

Simon snorted. 'I don't believe *that*, for a start.'

'Why ever not?'

'All immigrants are poor,' Simon said scornfully. 'Everyone knows that. That's why they come here.'

'He might have got rich since he came.'

Simon shrugged his shoulders.

'D'you mean Krishna's telling *lies*?'

'Well, not exactly. More that his Uncle is.'

'How d'you mean?'

Simon didn't answer for a minute. He slouched along, hands in pockets, forehead creased. Then he said slowly, 'I expect he's *got* an Uncle all right, but all that about him being rich and having a Cadillac is just nonsense! I expect what's happened is that his Uncle's written home, telling lies about how rich he is, and boasting . . . People *do* that sort of thing, sometimes! Make things up to look big . . .'

Mary, who should have known this was true if anyone did, felt indignant. 'It's you who's making things up! You don't *know*, do you? I think you're *mean*. I've half a mind to tell Krishna what you said!'

'That 'ud be meaner still, wouldn't it? What I said was private. Between you and me.'

Mary looked at him, at his nice, honest, troubled eyes, and felt ashamed. She said, 'Is that why you said we couldn't send a letter? Because you don't think his Uncle lives where he says, and someone else might get hold of it?'

Simon nodded miserably. 'It's the sort of address he might make up. I expect he thinks everyone in London lives near Buckingham Palace.'

Simon was probably right, Mary thought. He seemed to know more than she did, about a lot of things. On the other hand, her parents' flat was in a block quite near the Palace, and *they* weren't so very rich! Buckingham Palace Terrace might be quite a poor street, after all . . .

'I could go and see,' she said. 'I could go to London tomorrow. I've got enough money in my Pig, and I can ask my Aunt for a picnic lunch and say I want to spend the day on the beach . . .'

Simon kicked at a stone on the pavement. 'It's a bit of a wild goose chase, isn't it? Suppose he isn't there?'

He looked so crushed and worried, so bowed down, as if he were carrying a great weight on his shoulders, that Mary felt impatient. 'Well, if he isn't, we're no worse off! Don't *worry*, Simon . . .'

And Poll who had stopped to wait for them, and had heard this, said suddenly, 'Old worry-guts. That's what our Mum calls him.'

'She says she don't know where he gets it from,' Annabel said.

When they got to Harbour View, Mary wondered too. It was clearly not the sort of house in which anyone worried very much about anything; certainly not about noise or muddle. The narrow hall was littered with prams and toys, a number of large cardboard boxes and a brimming bucket of water, as if someone had been setting up an obstacle race. The family were in the room at the back: the two babies, Simon's Mum and his Gran and a big man in shirt sleeves whom Mary

supposed was his father. With Simon and herself and Polly-
Anna, that made nine people, all squashed into one tiny room
round a big table and all shouting, both at the same time and at
the tops of their voices, in order to make themselves heard
above the radio, which was belting out military music from
what sounded like several brass bands. In spite of the shouting,
Mary couldn't hear what anyone said, but she must have been
introduced, because the three grown-ups nodded and smiled
at her, and Simon's Mum took a pile of rumpled clothes off an
extra chair and pulled it up to the table.

The table was laid—at least, it had been laid, but now the
older baby was crawling the length of it, picking up knives
and forks as she went and dropping them over the edge. The
only person who seemed concerned—or even to notice what
she was doing—was Simon, who picked her up and strapped
her in a high chair. There was a look of intense, frowning
concentration on his face as he did this, and gave her a spoon
to bang with before picking up the dropped cutlery, and Mary
thought that if you were the sort of person who liked things
tidy and in their place, this might be an uncomfortable house
to live in.

For herself, she found it very comfortable. No one told
her to wash her hands, or asked her what she had been doing
all morning. They just piled her plate with roast pork and
vegetables and went on shouting at each other, cheerfully
but quite inaudibly, until Simon got up and turned off the
radio.

'That's better,' his father said. 'Now we can hear ourselves
speak.'

'Silence is golden,' his mother said.

'Cheap, too,' Simon said. 'You just have to turn a switch.'

'I didn't notice it was on.' Simon's Mum winked at Mary.

She was a pale, thin, pretty woman in an apron, and she reminded Mary of someone, though she couldn't think who.

'Not till it was turned off!' Mr Trumpet said, and roared with laughter.

'You don't have to shout now,' Simon said. 'Not unless you want to exercise your lungs.'

But they all continued to talk at the tops of their voices.

'Got enough to eat, Ursula?' Simon's father said.

'She's not Ursula, she's *Mary*,' Poll shouted. 'She's a NORPHAN.'

'She hasn't got any brothers or sisters,' Anna said.

'Sometimes I wish I hadn't,' Simon said. 'Stop blowing in your milk, Poll, it's disgusting.'

His mother smiled at Mary and slipped a piece of extra juicy crackling on to her plate. Mary knew this was because she thought she was an orphan, and, though she smiled back, felt it would choke her.

Poll went on, noisily blowing bubbles and giving herself a milk moustache. Anna looked at Simon, and giggled.

'It's sordid.' He appealed to his mother. 'They've got terrible manners.'

'You can't keep on, dear,' she said.

Simon went red. He fidgeted in his chair and then burst out, 'But you don't *start*. You let them do what they like. Talking with their mouths full, spitting in their milk . . .'

'Simon,' his father said.

'Silly Simon,' Anna said. 'It's because Mary's come to dinner. He thinks she's the *Queen*.'

Poll cackled insanely and rocked backwards and forwards in her chair.

Simon drew in a long breath and went redder still. He looked as if he were going to explode.

'Simon, Simon, Simon,' his father said.

Simon let the breath out, very slowly and gently. He stood up, not looking at anyone, and began to collect the empty plates. He carried them from the room, closing the door with his foot.

'He thinks we let him down.' Simon's father shook his head and pretended to wipe a tear from his eye.

'Hoity-toity,' his Gran said. She pulled a comic face, squinting down her nose like a shocked duchess, and the twins giggled, their cheeks shiny and solid as polished apples, and their glasses of milk bumping against their teeth.

'I'm sure I don't know where he gets his ideas from,' Mrs Trumpet said. 'Mary will just have to take us as she finds us, won't you, Mary?'

Mary was not sure how to reply, so she just smiled. She thought, privately, that they were a bit mean, laughing at Simon behind his back, but when he came back, carrying an enormous apple pie, and his mother said, 'Bless you, love. Whatever would I do without you?' she knew they were kind and loving as well.

The pie was sugary brown on the top and oozing pale, slippery juice at the edges. Mary ate a large wedge with yellow cream, and then had a second helping. When she was offered a third, she shook her head, regretfully.

'Are you sure you've had enough, dear?' Mrs Trumpet asked —almost as anxiously as Aunt Alice might have done.

'Quite sure, thank you,' Mary said. 'I couldn't eat another thing.'

And as soon as she had spoken she realised that she would have to. She looked at her watch. It was just after one o'clock now, and at half past, she would have to sit down and eat another lunch.

'Are you all right, dear?' Mrs Trumpet said. 'You look quite pale.'

Half an hour later, Aunt Alice said exactly the same thing.
'Are you all right, dear? You look quite pale.'
Mary looked at the plate of roast pork in front of her, blonde meat and crisp, brown crackling, and felt her stomach heave.
Try as she might, she could only pick at her plate.
'I knew you shouldn't have had those sandwiches!' Aunt Alice lamented.
Her grandfather looked over his spectacles. 'You know, Mary, a lot of children would be glad of that good dinner! Starving children in Africa!'
'I wish you'd give it to them, then,' Mary said—and thought of one child from Africa, who, though not exactly starving, was certainly hungry enough to enjoy her plate of roast pork. 'Pack it up and send it in a parcel!' she said, and the thought that this was just what they could do, if they only knew, made her laugh.
Once she had started, it was impossible to stop. She spattered half-chewed pork and potatoes all over Aunt Alice's beautifully polished table. She thought she would die, laughing . . .

EIGHT

The Wild Goose Chase

MONDAY MORNING WAS so bright and hot that even Aunt Alice could think of no objection when Mary asked if she might take a picnic lunch on the beach.

She did say, to Mary's horror, 'We might join you, dear, it's such a lovely day,' but luckily Grandfather sneezed twice at breakfast and Aunt Alice decided it might be unwise, in case he was getting a cold.

So as soon as breakfast was over, Mary went to the railway station. She had enough money for the return fare, and twenty two shillings and eightpence over, which she hoped would be enough to pay for a taxi from Victoria.

The meter had clocked up only two and sixpence when the taxi stopped in a street of tall, white houses with big windows and imposing front porches.

'Are you sure this is the right address?' Mary said, and the taxi driver shrugged his shoulders.

'It's the one you give me, Miss.'

He was a sour-faced man with a red lump, like a small plum, on the side of his nose. When Mary got out and paid him the exact fare on the meter, he looked sourer still. She gave him the two spare pennies from her purse and said, 'Thank you for your kindness,' which was something she had heard her grandfather say, when he gave someone a tip. The taxi driver looked at the pennies. Then he grinned suddenly, said, 'Thank *you*, Your Ladyship,' flicked up his *For Hire* sign, and drove away.

Mary looked at Number Four, Buckingham Palace Terrace. A flight of marble steps led up to a solid, shining, black door. At the side was a row of bells, each with a polished, brass grille beside it. Mary climbed the steps slowly. She knew she had to press a bell and speak into the grille, and somehow this was far more frightening than knocking on a door and waiting for someone to come.

There were five bells. There were no names beside four of them, but the bottom bell was marked *Housekeeper*. Mary hesitated; then she pressed this bell, very gently.

Nothing happened. She waited a minute, and then she pressed again. This time a door in the basement area opened, and someone said, ' 'Allo?'

Mary looked over the side of the steps. An alarming woman stood there; very tall, with long, black hair, a great, hooked nose, and a black patch over one eye. Like a female pirate, Mary thought. She looked at Mary with a fierce expression.

Mary said, 'Does Mr Patel live here?'

The woman shook her head. 'Not understand,' she said.

Mary spoke slowly. 'Mr Patel. He's—he's a black man.'

The woman shook her head again. She smiled, showing a lot of gold teeth. The smile made her look even more alarming. She said, 'Come,' and beckoned to Mary. Then she turned to the door of the basement flat, and, as Mary came down the steps, she could hear her speaking in a foreign language to someone inside. Mary lingered for a minute, afraid to follow the woman down to the basement, and began to feel self-conscious and foolish. Of course Simon was right! She had known it, really, as soon as the taxi stopped! This was far too rich and grand a neighbourhood for a poor immigrant to live!

Simon was so sure he must be poor, and had written home, boasting . . .

Or perhaps Krishna had been lying, after all! He was quite capable of it: the account he had given them of his journey to England was too exciting to be altogether true . . . His Rich Uncle was probably like her Wicked Aunt, Mary thought; a story he had been making up.

Once she had decided this, she felt panicky. Suppose that forbidding, dark door were to open, and someone come out? Someone who would scream, *What do you think you're doing, ringing bells and bothering people? Of course there are no poor immigrants here* . . .

Mary called 'Thank you', down to the basement, but no one seemed to hear. She began to walk away, and then a foolish fear snapped at her heels, and made her run.

So by the time the two Portuguese women in the basement had decided that the little girl must mean the Indian gentleman in the top flat, she had turned the corner and was out of sight . . .

Mary's parents' flat was in a big block near Hyde Park. Mary went up in the lift and got out her key which she always kept in a zipped pocket at the back of her purse. For a minute, just before she opened the door, she felt quite excited to be coming home . . .

But the feeling didn't last. Once she was inside, it didn't feel like home at all. Not like anybody's home. The narrow hall was dark and cold and there was a curious, shut-up smell; both sweet and stale; a mixture of polish and dust.

There were letters on the mat. Mary stirred them with her foot to see if there was anything interesting, but there were only dull, type-written envelopes. Just circulars and bills, she thought, and suddenly, in her mind, she could hear her father's voice.

Bills, bills, nothing but bills . . .

It was one of the things he said almost every morning at breakfast. When she was younger, Mary had thought they must be dreadfully poor, but as she had grown older she realised that he only complained about money in order to annoy her mother, just as her mother only complained about the dull life she led in order to annoy *him*. Sometimes her mother would take no notice when he talked about the bills, and would go on, calmly drinking her coffee and reading the newspaper as if he wasn't even in the room, but sometimes she would get angry and shout at him, and say, what did he expect? Things had to be paid for, didn't they? And then her father would shout back until her mother got up and went out, slamming the door . . .

Mary sighed. She thought it was really much more comfortable living with Grandfather and Aunt Alice, and then she felt ashamed of thinking like that, and sighed again.

She opened the door into the living room. The blinds were down, and it was as chilly and depressing as the hall. The furniture was there, in its place, but someone had taken all the pictures away, leaving marks on the walls, and the books had gone from the shelves. Mary shivered—but not because she was cold. The room was so empty. It was like a display room in a furniture shop. As if no one had ever lived here. Or would ever live here again . . .

Her parents' bedroom opened off the living room. A dust-sheet covered the bed and the wardrobe door stood open. Mary looked inside and saw that everything had gone. Their clothes, their shoes . . .

She caught her breath and ran to her own room, flinging

the door wide. For several minutes she stood quite still, looking round her. Nothing had gone from here; everything was where she had left it, her rocking horse, her desk, her books, her toys—all her precious possessions—but for some reason none of them seemed to be anything to do with her. It was as if they belonged to someone else. To a girl in a story.

It was a peculiar and frightening feeling. She gave a sudden, loud laugh to try and shake it off, and tapped the rocking horse on his nose to set him moving. As he rocked, creaking, she remembered how she had ridden him last winter, when her parents were out, holding a wriggling, spitting Noakes on the crupper, to keep her company.

She said 'Noakes,' and ran to the kitchen. This was the nicest room in the flat, with yellow walls and a big window that looked on to the fire escape. There was a cat door fixed in one of the panes so that Noakes could come and go as he pleased.

She called him again but without much hope. She knew his habits. He roamed wild all night and most of the day, only coming home in the late afternoon for his meal, which he slept off in the early part of the evening before he went out again. Mary's mother had promised to ask a neighbour to come in while they were away, and feed him daily.

So though Mary called 'Noakes' once more, she didn't really expect an answer. And when one came, it was so thin and faint that she wasn't sure if she had really heard it.

Then there was another mew. She turned, and saw a thin shape, dragging itself from under the gas stove.

She stared. She could hardly believe her eyes. It was Noakes —but a Noakes so changed! His glossy coat was dull and dusty and he limped on three legs, one front paw drawn up beneath him. She knelt down and he rubbed against her leg, purring rustily. She stroked him—and it was like stroking a skeleton.

She looked round the kitchen and saw his feeding bowls, one for milk and one for meat. They were both empty and covered with a sticky film of dust. She said, 'Damn. Oh *damn* her,' but though she was angry, she wasn't, in her heart, surprised. It was only what she might have expected. Her mother had forgotten. She had been so busy packing to go away, that Noakes had gone from her mind.

Not that it would have mattered, in the ordinary way. A cat like Noakes could normally keep himself sleek and fat on mice and birds and dustbin pickings. But not if he were ill. Not with a damaged leg!

'Oh Noakes, darling Noakes,' she mourned, and picked him up, alarmed to find that he not only let her do this, but lay quite still in her arms.

She held him for a minute, then put him gently down.

'You just want something to eat,' she said, 'then you'll feel better.'

She found a tin of condensed milk in the larder. She opened it, diluted a spoonful with water, and poured it into a saucer. But when she put it beside him, he made no move at all.

'Come on,' she coaxed. 'Come on, silly boy.' She lifted him on to her lap and tried to spoon the milk into his mouth, but most of it dribbled out again, streaking his fur and running over her hand.

She said, speaking angrily because she was frightened, 'If you don't eat, you old fool, you'll *die*,' and he moved his head then and rasped some of the spilled milk off her finger with his rough tongue, almost as if he understood her.

'There, ' she said admiringly—and in much the same tone of voice that Aunt Alice used when Mary had eaten up all her rice pudding—'*Wasn't* that nice?' She dipped her finger into the milk for him to lick it. A lot got spilled that way, but a little went inside him, and she thought he looked better. When she put him down, he sat up groggily, and began to clean the sticky patches off his fur.

She hunted for his travelling basket, finding it full of dirty dusters and tins of polish, in the bottom of a cupboard. She tipped the tins and the dusters out on the floor and lined the basket with a clean towel. She would have to take him back with her and Aunt Alice would have to put up with it! She might not like cats, but she wouldn't turn Noakes away, not once he was actually there, and she might not even want to, now he was so ill. She liked fussing over people, and Noakes needed fussing over . . .

The only trouble was that when she turned up with Noakes they would know she had been to London. And though she could explain that she had suddenly wanted to see Noakes quite terribly, and they might understand that, they would both be hurt because she had sneaked off without telling them.

Particularly Aunt Alice! She would probably cry and say, 'Mary doesn't trust me! Oh—it's my fault. I should have offered to have the cat in the first place!'

Settling Noakes in the basket, Mary groaned aloud. It was a shame to upset Aunt Alice, even though she was so silly. But it couldn't be helped: Noakes came first.

And the first thing she had to do for him, was to take him to the vet.

The vet said, 'He's taken quite a battering, hasn't he? Had an argument with a car, I should think.'

Noakes lay on the table, limp and still. He looked more like a shabby fur collar than a cat. He had squeaked once, when the vet touched his leg. Since then, he had made no further sound.

Mary said, 'Last time I brought him, you had to tie him in a blanket before he'd let you look at him! And even then, he managed to scratch you!'

'Did he? Well he's past that now, I'm afraid. Poor old chap.'

'Noakes isn't old,' Mary said. 'He's just been in a lot of fights. He's a terrible fighter. That's how he tore his ear and lost his eye.'

'Some of his teeth, too,' the vet said. 'It seems he's led a pretty full life. Nine full lives, in fact. You know, I rather think . . .' He stopped. 'Do you think you could leave him here, and ask your mother to come and see me?'

'My mother is dead,' Mary said, without a pause.

'Oh. I see.' The vet looked doubtfully at Mary. It was perhaps half a minute before she understood what was in his mind. Then all the blood seemed to rush into her head and she felt sick and dizzy with anger. She wanted to fly at him, and kick and punch him, but she didn't. She held on to the side of the table and managed to speak coldly and calmly.

'I brought him to be made better. Not to be *murdered*!'

'Well. Yes. I understand that,' the vet said. He sounded uncomfortable. 'It's just that sometimes it's kinder . . .'

He wasn't looking at Mary now. He was feeling Noakes very carefully and gently and his eyes were half closed, as if he were trying to concentrate on the message his fingers were sending him.

Mary drew a deep breath. She wanted him to help Noakes, so it was no good losing her temper.

'He's awfully strong, really. Honestly, I know he looks bad now, but he's got a very strong constitution.'

The vet didn't answer.

Mary said, 'You wouldn't kill someone you knew, would you? Not a person. I mean, he's just a cat to you, but he's Noakes to me.'

To stop herself crying, she thought of her mother, going away on holiday and leaving Noakes to starve.

She thought—If Noakes dies, I'll never speak to her again!

She said passionately, 'If you don't know how to make him better, then just say so! I'll take him away and find someone who can!'

The vet looked up, startled, and at the same moment Noakes whipped his head round and bit the side of his thumb. The vet swore and then, unexpectedly, grinned.

'All right,' he said. 'He's got a bit of fight in him yet. But I'll have to take that stump off. It's not doing him any good. Just a source of infection. I can't promise he'll live, mind. But it'll give him a chance, as long as he's looked after. He's been rather neglected up to now, hasn't he?'

Mary nodded. She could have explained that it wasn't her fault, but it didn't seem important. Her chest felt tight and sore and her eyes were burning. 'I'll look after him from now on,' she whispered, 'I promise.'

She sat in the waiting room, on a hard-backed chair, hugging her arms round her chest and gabbling under her breath. *Please God, if you let Noakes get better, I'll be good for the rest of my life. I mean, I'll try to be good. Let him get better. Please . . .*

There was a clock on the wall. It had a big, red, second hand that seemed to crawl round. A minute on that clock was more like an hour, Mary thought.

She watched the clock and continued to chant in a low voice. *Please God, let Noakes get well, let him get well and I'll try to be good . . .*

She felt that if she stopped for so much as a second, Noakes might die now, under the anaesthetic.

Let Noakes get better, let Noakes get better . . .

When the vet opened the door, he saw her moving lips and coughed, to warn her he was there. She slid off the chair and stood facing him, ramrod straight, like a soldier on parade.

He said, 'All over now. It wasn't as bad a job as I thought. He'll be all right, I think.'

Mary followed him into the surgery. There was a sweetish smell in the air. Noakes was lying in his basket and there was a bandage where his leg had been.

The vet said, 'Now. He'll just sleep it off. No need to feed him until tomorrow, unless he'll take a little milk. But then you must feed him regularly. Something light to begin with— a raw egg, beaten up in milk with perhaps a drop of brandy. You don't have to touch the wound. The bandage'll drop off when it's healed.'

Mary said, 'How much do I owe you?'

She knew she ought to say *thank you*, but she felt too stiff and awkward.

The vet didn't seem to mind. He smiled. 'Ten and six be all right?'

Mary hesitated. Ten and six was what they charged just for a consultation. She was sure it should be more than that. She said, 'I've got a pound. You can have my pound, if you like.'

'I think ten and six is quite enough,' the vet said.

All the way home, she held the basket on her lap, steadying it against the joggling of the train. There was no one else in the carriage and she talked to Noakes softly, in case he should wake up and wonder where he was.

'It's all right, Noakes. I'm here. I'm looking after you. It's all right, Noakes ...'

Once she opened the lid of the basket. He was still uncon-
scious—or asleep—but when she touched his hard, wedge-
shaped head, he flicked his ear against her finger.

Simon was waiting at the station. She could see him dodging
about behind some other people on the far side of the barrier.
He pounced on her as soon as she was through. 'You've been
ages, I've met two trains already,' he accused her. 'Did you
find him?'

Mary's mind was full of Noakes. She said happily, 'I've
got him with me, in the basket. Oh Simon . . .'

'*What?*'

'I'm sorry I'm late, but I had to take him to the vet.'

'The *vet?*' he repeated, and stared at her as if she had suddenly
gone mad.

She realised that he was talking about Krishna's Uncle, and
began to laugh at the thought of taking an Indian gentleman to
the vet and bringing him home in a basket! She laughed so
much that water came into her eyes. 'I mean my *cat*. My cat,
Noakes. I couldn't find Uncle Patel. He wasn't there. You
were right about that!'

She was so happy at this moment that she didn't mind ad-
mitting this.

'Oh God,' Simon said bleakly. He turned on his heel and
walked fast out of the station yard, hands in pockets, head
down.

Mary ran after him. She thought—What an impossible
boy! First he said there was no point in her going to London,
and now, when he was proved right, he was sulking about
it!

She said, 'You didn't expect me to find him, did you? I
mean, you said it was just a wild goose chase.'

He nodded briefly, looking pale and harassed. 'I just

hoped . . .' he said, and then his voice trailed away, as if he were too miserable to say any more.

She said, 'What's the matter with you? All right—so I couldn't find his Uncle! It's not the end of the world, is it? We'll just have to look after him a bit longer, that's all. Until . . .'

'Until *what*?' Simon said. His eyes had gone dark.

She couldn't think, so she tossed her head. 'Well, until something happens, that's all . . .'

She thought she was glad she hadn't found Uncle Patel. If she had, he would have come and taken Krishna away. And then everything would be as it had been before—dreadfully boring and dull.

Simon said slowly, 'Something *has* happened. That's the trouble. My Uncle Horace is coming home tomorrow. Mum had a letter this morning.'

NINE

The Flight to the Island

'WE'VE GOT TO think of somewhere to hide him,' Mary said, for the twentieth time in an hour. 'We've just got to!'

'Oh don't keep on,' Simon said. 'What d'you think I'm trying to do?'

His indignation sounded put-on. Mary looked at him, puzzled, but he avoided her eyes and slumped into a crouched, defeated position, arms dangling, head sunk forward.

Krishna had been sitting on the floor watching Noakes, who was beginning to stir awake in his basket. Now he looked at this picture of gloom and said, sadly and politely, 'I am sorry. I am a great worry for Simon.'

'It's not your fault,' Mary said crossly. 'It's him. It's the way he's made. Silly old worry-guts Simon.'

She thought he was really unbearably stupid! So *dull*— turning what should be fun and excitement into trouble and fuss, as if he were a boring grown-up instead of a boy! Why, they were *lucky* to have an adventure like this! Krishna was a refugee from a stupid, silly law. You didn't find a real, live refugee to rescue every day. Simon ought to be glad of the chance . . .

'Feeble spasticated twit,' she said, and jabbed him in the ribs, so that he toppled over.

He said furiously, 'I suppose you think there's nothing to worry about.'

'Not as much as you make out.'

Krishna said, 'I can go to London myself, to look for my Uncle. Then I will be no more trouble to you.'

The stupidity of this remark drew Mary and Simon together. They looked at each other with resigned expressions. Krishna seemed to have no idea of the danger he was in! When they tried to explain, he just yawned and looked bored. It was difficult to know what he thought—if, indeed, he thought anything! Perhaps the truth was he had had such a frightening time since he left Africa that his mind had gone numb— *frozen over*, Mary thought, so that everything they told him just skated over the surface, leaving no mark.

'You can't go to London,' she said. 'We told you. Your Uncle doesn't live where you said, so there's no way to find him. And you can't just go wandering round London, looking. You'd be caught and put in prison.'

Krishna didn't answer. From the look of him, Mary thought, he was un-focusing his eyes, the way she did when someone said something she didn't want to listen to. Then he turned away and stretched out his hand towards Noakes.

'I shouldn't touch him,' Mary warned, but she was too late. He was already tickling the cat, behind his good ear.

Noakes stretched, arching his back. Then he began to purr, like an engine.

Mary felt jealous. 'He wouldn't have let you do that, if he was well.'

'He looks awful,' Simon said. 'Moth-eaten. Are you sure your Aunt'll let you keep him? I mean, if she's so beastly, won't she just say what the vet did? That he ought to be put down?'

Mary said helplessly, 'I don't know . . .' Then she thought that even the real Aunt Alice might react just as the vet had done. Not because she was wicked, but because she was kind. The vet had said *Sometimes it's kinder in the long run* . . .

She said, 'He'll get better. I know he will.'

'He could stay here with me,' Krishna said. 'I have never had a cat for a pet. At home we have only dogs—and ostriches in our Zoo in the garden.'

'And lions and tigers too, no doubt,' Mary said, and grinned at Simon.

Krishna looked surprised. 'No, it is only a small, private Zoo. And there are no tigers in Africa, didn't you know that? But we have a leopard cub and some chameleons and the ostriches. *Please* let Noakes stay. It is so lonely at night, on my own.'

Mary hesitated. She had made up her mind, but didn't want to give in too easily. 'Oh all right,' she said grudgingly, and was rewarded by Krishna's smile, so broad and white that it seemed to split his face in two. She went on, 'But only for tonight, mind. We'll have to see about tomorrow.'

Tomorrow . . . the word plopped between them like a stone in a pond, and spread ripples. Mary looked at Simon who stared into space.

Krishna said, 'Where will I go tomorrow, Simon? When your Uncle Horace comes?'

He sounded interested, not anxious at all. Simon looked at his trusting face and sighed, a long, deep sigh. Then he said, 'Somewhere you'll be good and safe. I'll take you first thing in the morning.'

He spoke so calmly and casually, that it took Mary's breath away for a minute. When she had recovered she said, 'You've known where to go all along, haven't you? Why didn't you say?'

Simon looked at his feet. One big toe was poking through a

hole in his canvas shoe. He wiggled it up and down, keeping his eyes fixed on it, as if a wiggling toe was the most fascinating sight in the world. 'I thought I might think of somewhere else. You see, this place I mean is private.'

'D'you mean, Trespassers Will Be Prosecuted?'

How like Simon, Mary thought, to worry about a little thing like that!

Understanding her, he flushed darkly. 'Well, of course it's that too. But what I meant was, private to *me*. No one else knows about it. And I sort of wanted to keep it . . .'

'Is it a nice place, Simon?' Krishna asked.

Simon watched his wiggling toe. 'It is the most beautiful place in the world,' he said in a hoarse voice.

Then he blinked rapidly and nervously as if he had been caught out in something shameful, clapped his hands on his knees and jumped up. 'Quarter to nine tomorrow,' he said to Mary. 'Bus stop by the pier. And bring all the food you can carry.'

Mary got up very early the next morning, to raid the larder. She took a few tins, a loaf of bread, a carton of eggs and some brandy for Noakes, taken from Grandfather's private supply and poured into an empty Schweppes Tonic Water bottle with a screw lid. She filled a carrier bag and put it ready in the bushes by the front gate.

When Aunt Alice came down, Mary asked if she could have a picnic, like yesterday.

Aunt Alice took half a cold chicken out of the larder and got out the carving knife.

'I could eat all of that,' Mary said.

Aunt Alice looked at her, knife poised. 'There's quite a lot of meat on it, dear. Waste not, want not, you know.'

She gave one of her loud, merry laughs to show that she didn't really grudge Mary the chicken, if she wanted it.

'I shan't waste it,' Mary said.

So she got the chicken and some beetroot sandwiches, two apples, three bananas, a box of Garibaldi biscuits, a bottle of milk and a fat wedge of pale, cheddar cheese.

'Somebody's eye is bigger than her stomach,' Aunt Alice said.

'Well, there's my friend,' Mary said. 'His mother might not give him enough.'

She had discovered long ago that it was best to tell people a little of the truth: it stopped them being suspicious. 'His name's Simon Trumpet,' she said. 'He's an awfully nice boy.'

'Trumpet, Trumpet . . .' Aunt Alice said. 'Now where have I heard that name before?'

'His father's a policeman,' Mary said, thinking this sounded very respectable. And his Uncle's got a shop in the town. Horace Trumpet. Antiques.'

'I know. A fat man with a beard. But it wasn't him I was thinking about.' Aunt Alice pursed her lips, trying to remember. Then she gave up and said, 'I hope you're not going to carry that picnic too far, dear. You'll strain your stomach.'

'It's not heavy,' Mary said, setting down the duffel bag in which she had been packing the food, and smiling at her Aunt.

The duffel bag might not be heavy, but the carrier bag with the tins was a different matter. By the time Mary had got to the pier and lugged her burdens on to the top deck of the bus, she was hot and sweating. Simon and Krishna were already there; a bulky rucksack and Noakes's basket parked on the seat in front of them.

'Noakes slept on my chest all night,' Krishna said proudly.

'I think he likes me. And he is much better. When Simon came this morning, we gave him some milk and he drank every bit.'

'Did anyone see you leave the shop?' Mary whispered, but Simon frowned at her. The conductor had followed Mary up the stairs and was standing just behind her, waiting for their fares.

Mary's heart thumped, but the conductor barely glanced at Krishna who looked, in fact, quite ordinary in Mary's sweater and some old jeans of Simon's.

All the same, as the bus filled up, it seemed best to keep quiet. Only Krishna spoke, once, when they had left the town and were jolting inland. He said, 'My Uncle told me England was very green.'

They got off on a busy, main road. Cars rushed past them and huge lorries, spraying sand and ballast. There was a high stone wall on their right, grim and forbidding with broken glass on the top. Simon led them along a little way to a rusty, iron gate. Creepers had tangled over it, and the silky weed called old man's beard, almost hiding a faded notice that was tied to the bars with wire. PRIVATE ESTATE. KEEP OUT.

The gate was padlocked and chained, but uselessly: its hinges were broken. Simon gave one expert heave, and the gate fell back, leaving a space big enough for them to squeeze through. Then he closed it behind them.

Once inside, the noisy road might not have existed. A few yards from the gate, they were in a different world; a hushed, green jungle. Trees, crowded together and grown tall and spindly, met overhead and shut out the sky. The ground was a tangle of spiky brambles that tore at their clothes.

'This way,' Simon said, and set off confidently, though there seemed no obvious path. Krishna and Mary stumbled after him, Krishna carrying the cat basket, and Mary the two bags of food. Invisible cobwebs brushed their faces. Simon was going too fast for them, but they had no breath to complain.

After what seemed ages, he stopped in a small clearing, shafted with smoky sunlight and whirring with crickets.

'My *leg*,' Krishna said, and bent to unravel a bramble that had snaked up under his jeans. As he pulled out the thorns, a row of blood dots appeared, like small beads.

'There aren't many more brambles,' Simon said. 'That's the worst bit, 'cept for the nettles. Give me one of those bags, Mary, you'll need a free hand.'

When he led the way out of the clearing, she saw what he meant. There was a path now, though very narrow and over-grown. It went down, along the side of a steep hill; the earth was damp and squidgy underfoot, and nettles, tall as they were, whipped at their faces. It was so quiet, they could hear themselves breathing.

'Watch out, there's a bit of a tree fallen,' Simon said. 'Look, that's where it came from.'

They looked up and saw the tree high above them, a white scar down the side where the great branch had torn away. It was slimy with moss, and dangerous. Simon crossed first, and then turned to take the cat basket, for safety's sake. There was no sound from inside.

'I suppose he's all right,' Mary said. 'Ought we to look?'

'He's just sleeping sound,' Simon said. 'We'll let him out when we get to the island.'

'What island?' Mary said, and, as if in answer, the trees on the right thinned out and they could see water beyond, covered in bright green weed, like a curly mat.

'It's an artificial lake,' Simon explained. 'There used to be a big house on the other side, but it burned down ages ago, and the people went away and never came back ...'

The path came down to the lake, and was easier walking now. They turned a bend and saw the island, so thick with trees and huge, sprawling rhododendrons that it looked as if it would be impossible to land there. There was no weed on this part of the lake; a humped, wooden bridge spanned a stretch of brown, glinting water.

Simon said, 'The bridge is tricky. I'll take the rucksack first.'

They followed him on to the first half of the bridge where the planks were rotten and shuggly, but held them. The second half was almost gone. Only a single beam remained, about five inches wide.

The water underneath was running fast. Mary looked down and felt giddy. 'It's shallow,' she said. 'Can't we wade instead?'

Simon shook his head. 'It's quick-mud. You'd be sucked down.'

He went across like a tight-rope walker and came back for the cat basket. Noakes had begun to stir, and thump against the sides. 'Leave the bags,' Simon said. 'You'll need your hands to balance.'

Even with nothing to carry, it was an alarming exercise. 'Don't look down,' Simon warned, as Mary took her first step on the beam, but she found it impossible not to. She saw the racing water and felt her stomach lurch. She said, terrified, 'I'll fall—*Simon* . . .' and at once he was there, coming halfway across the beam to take her hand and steady her. He led her safely across and called to Krishna, 'Come on, it's all right, really. Just that girls are hopeless at balancing.'

He winked at Mary, and she knew he wasn't sneering at her, just stiffening Krishna's pride.

It worked. Simon stood at one end of the beam and Krishna

walked straight across, his eyes fixed on his face. Safe on the island, he beamed with pleasure. 'I was not scared like you, Mary. It was *easy*.'

'Don't boast then,' Simon said. 'If something's naturally easy, it's nothing to boast about.'

He went back for the bags. Even to watch him, made Mary feel giddy, so she turned her back and opened the cat basket.

'Don't let him out now,' Simon said, putting the bags down. 'Wait till we get there.'

'Get where?'

'You'll see.'

Simon looked different, Mary thought. His worried look had gone and his eyes were bright as stars. He said, 'It's a marvellous place—you just wait and see!'

He was so excited and happy that Mary felt nervous for him. As they climbed up, across the island, she hoped that this place was as special as he believed it to be, so that she wouldn't have to pretend and hurt his feelings.

She didn't have to pretend. It was better than she could have imagined. They came down the side of a mossy bluff to a small inlet where the lake ran into a cave—but not an ordinary cave! The walls and arching roof were encrusted with millions of tiny, crystal spikes, glinting where the sun shone in and reflecting the moving water, so that they seemed to move and shimmer, the colour changing with the light, now purple, now pink, now gold. Off the main cave, up crooked, rocky steps and along twisting, narrow passages, were other caves, or chambers, each with its intricate pattern of crystals. Here and there clusters hung down, like swarming bees, or tiny chandeliers.

'It's a grotto,' Simon said. 'An artificial grotto. The people who owned the house built it—oh, about two hundred years ago. I read about it in an old book Uncle Horace had in his shop. They copied it from a real grotto, in Italy.'

'Why?' Krishna said.

'For fun, I suppose. For picnics. There's a landing stage in the main part, only it's rotted now.'

'They must have been fabulously rich,' Mary said. '*Billionaires*. Are these diamonds on the walls?'

Simon laughed. 'Only quartz, I think. It's brick underneath. You can see in the places where the crystals have come off.'

They walked round, marvelling. Simon led them into a higher chamber than the others, where the floor was dry, beaten earth and a grilled window let in a leafy, speckled light. In one corner there was a hole, covered with branches and full of tinned food—salmon, sardines, baked beans. 'I bought them with my newspaper round money,' Simon said. 'A few tins, every week. I thought we'd sleep here, Krishna. You'll be quite comfy. I've got my blanket and you can have my sleeping bag ...'

Krishna looked at Simon worshipfully. 'I am so glad you are staying too,' he said.

Simon glanced rather shyly at Mary. 'I told my Mum I was going camping. I often do, in the holidays. She didn't ask any questions.'

Mary said, 'You didn't tell *me*, did you? Not that I *care* ...'

Her throat had begun to ache. It was so unfair. *She* had found Krishna and rescued him, and now they had arranged this between them, plotting behind her back. Boys were all the same. They would make friends with a girl if there was no one else around, but as soon as another boy came along, they were off and away ...

'I'd better go and feed Noakes, I think,' she said, and walked straight-backed out of the chamber, down to the main cave.

She got out milk, eggs and brandy, and mixed them in a billy with a stick. She hummed a cheerful tune, so that Simon would think she was quite happy.

He came and stood behind her, watching Noakes who was balancing uncertainly on his three legs, and lapping at the milk.

'I'm sorry,' he said, at length.

'Sorry for what?' Mary put on an astonished face.

'You know . . .'

Mary shrugged her shoulders. 'Two's company, I suppose.' Her eyes were smarting.

'T'isn't that.' Simon squatted beside her. 'I had to, didn't I? I mean, I couldn't leave him alone, not to begin with. And there wasn't time to explain, last night . . .' He paused. 'You could stay, too. I was going to suggest that. If you want to run away from your Aunt. As she's so foul . . .'

He was looking at her rather oddly, Mary thought. As if he were testing her, or something . . .

What could she say? Not, 'Aunt Alice would worry.' That would sound silly.

She found an answer. 'She'd set the police on to me. Then we'd none of us be safe.'

'They'd never track you here. I wish you would. It would be more fun with you.'

Mary's heart lightened. 'T'isn't worth risking,' she said firmly. 'And I can come every day and bring milk, and anything you want. I'd be more useful, that way.'

He nodded, accepting this. 'You can always change your mind,' he said.

After that, it was a perfect day. They built a fire in the clearing above the bluff, and baked some potatoes Simon had brought with him. They were a bit charred and flaky, as they didn't wait for the fire to burn down to the right kind of glowing ash, but they went down very nicely with lashings of butter, and cold chicken, and the beetroot sandwiches. They drank the bottle of milk and ate the Garibaldi biscuits and the cheese and the fruit; then, stomachs tight as drums, lay on their backs and went to sleep in the sun.

When they woke, Noakes, who had shared the chicken and then curled up in his basket, had vanished. They found him, stalking a grasshopper on the edge of the clearing, crouching low and moving silkily and expertly as if he had been used to balancing on three legs all his life.

Simon bent to touch him and he growled and spat and arched his back like a wild cat. Simon drew back hastily and Mary laughed. This was the old Noakes, come back!

'He's better,' she said. 'Better already. It's like magic.'

Simon went pink. 'It's a magic place,' he said shyly and earnestly. 'I always felt that. Anyone 'ud get well here.'

'My foot's well,' Krishna said. 'It was hurting on the walk, but it is better now.' He unwound the bandage and stretched out his ankle. 'I feel like playing a game.' he announced. 'A running, jumping, *playing* game.'

And they did. They ran, and whooped, and shouted, and laughed, and climbed trees, and splashed in and out of the lake. They were really very silly. Mary hung upside down from a tree and pulled the most frightful faces and Krishna laughed, high and shrill, like a bird. Mary realised she had only heard him laugh like that once before—when she had fallen into the dustbin in the alley. She dropped from the tree and chased him, making madder and madder faces, until he fell in a heap on the ground and clutched his stomach and cried, 'Stop I shall *die*.'

Simon, who was usually so sober and quiet and responsible.

made most noise of all. He yelled and screamed and stood on his head, waggling his heels in the air.

He behaved like someone who had been shut up for ages—and suddenly set free.

When they were quite exhausted, they sat down by the remains of the fire, and stretched and yawned.

'I like it here,' Krishna said. 'It is the best place I have ever been. I am glad I came to England. You are so kind to me.'

'I wish I was sure we were being kind,' Simon said, a little later on. It was time for Mary to go home and he had come with her as far as the road, leaving Krishna behind on the island, to keep the fire going and look after Noakes.

'I mean, hiding him,' Simon said. 'I wish I was sure that was the right thing.'

Mary said nothing. She was thinking about Noakes who had followed them as far as the bridge, but stayed behind when they crossed, watching them and switching his tail. Mary wondered if he thought she had abandoned him.

'I mean,' Simon said slowly, 'there's usually two ways of looking at something. Looked at *one* way, you could say we were rescuers . . .'

'Aren't we?' Mary said.

'Well. *I* think we are—at least, I *think* we are—and *you* think we are, but some people might think different.' Simon paused for a minute, frowning. Then he said. 'Some people might think we looked more like kidnappers!'

It was queer, Mary thought. On the island, Simon had behaved like a normal boy without a care in the world, but now, as soon as he had left it, he had started being solemn again, weighing things up and worrying over nothing.

'I think you're just *ridiculous*,' she said.

Later that evening, though, something happened to make
her think again.

She had had her bath after supper and come down to say
goodnight. Grandfather was watching the television news, and
Aunt Alice put her finger on her lips to warn Mary to keep
quiet.

Mary settled down at her feet, feeling pleasantly sleepy—so
sleepy, indeed, that she actually leaned her head against Aunt
Alice's boney knee and felt very comfortable there.

Aunt Alice kept very still.

Mary didn't listen to the news. She closed her eyes and let
the sound drift over her head. It was only because Grandfather
said, 'That's enough. Turn it off, Mary dear, my bones feel old
tonight,' that she heard the last item.

She had her hand on the switch when the announcer said,
'There is no further news of the boy, Krishna Patel, who disappeared from the London bound charter flight from Nairobi.
His Uncle, with whom the boy was expected to stay in England,
flew to Paris this morning to assist the French police in their
enquiries. At the Airport, Mr Patel said . . .'

Mary turned the knob, silencing Uncle Patel. After the first,
stunned moment, she felt quite calm. *Just as well Simon didn't
hear that*, was all she consciously thought.

She turned round, smiling, and turned the smile into a yawn.

'You look tired, dear,' Aunt Alice said. 'I hope you didn't
overdo things today.'

'I had a lovely time,' Mary said. 'I'm having a lovely time
all the time now. I want it to go on and on . . .'

'Is there any reason why it shouldn't dear?' Aunt Alice said.

TEN

The Best Place in the World

AND THE GOOD time did go on. Each day dawned bright and still and so hot that the dew dried before breakfast. The first day on the island, the second, the third . . . After a week, Mary lost count of time; the days seemed to slip, like warm sand, through her fingers.

If her conscience troubled her, it was only the merest twinge, and only at the beginning, when she had thought *what would Simon do if he knew?*—and decided that he would write to Uncle Patel at the address Krishna had given them. They still couldn't be sure he lived there, of course, but Simon would say they ought to try, just the same.

She had written a letter one morning, using block capitals— YOUR NEPHEW IS IN GOOD HANDS, HAVE NO FEAR FOR HIS SAFETY—and signed it, A FRIEND. But after looking at it for a while, she had torn it into little pieces and flushed it down the lavatory. If she sent it, the postmark would give a clue, and the police might come, looking.

The island was the safest and most secret place imaginable, but there was a risk. And even the smallest risk wasn't worth taking.

It wasn't just that *she* wanted the adventure to go on and on! Krishna was better off on the island, living free and running wild, than he would be in prison. And even if they didn't put him in prison, but let him live with his Uncle, stuffy old

London was almost as bad as prison, in weather like this. Mary remembered hot summer days in the flat, with nothing to do and nowhere to go except the Park and shopping with her mother.

Perhaps if her parents had been different sort of people, Mary might have thought how Krishna's must be feeling, not knowing where their son was, or even if he were alive and well. But Mary's father didn't write, and although her mother sent her postcards from time to time, Mary knew this didn't mean a thing. Everyone sent postcards when they went on holiday, and often to people they didn't care about at all! *Darling,* Mary's mother wrote, *this is such a lovely place, I wish you were here*—but of course, if Mary were there, her mother would be bored to tears! As bored as Mary herself would be, trailing round foreign shops and cafes and having to wear her best clothes and be polite to the dull people her mother made friends with.

Children were a nuisance to parents, Mary considered, and parents a nuisance to children. They were better off apart from each other.

If Simon thought differently, if he worried sometimes about Krishna's parents, he kept it to himself. Perhaps the truth was that deep down he was more frightened than Mary of what they were doing, and so, quite deliberately, didn't think about it; just lived for the moment and was happy.

'Simon is much nicer now,' Krishna said one day.

They had just finished lunch; Simon was digging earth-worms somewhere, and Krishna was fishing. This was a pleasantly idle occupation, suitable for a hot afternoon and a full stomach: Krishna had thrown out the line with a bunch of worms on the hook, taken a half hitch round a tin can perched on a pile of stones, tied the end to his ankle, and now lay comfortably on his back, watching the sky.

'What d'you mean? Simon's always nice,' Mary felt obliged to say, though she was too sleepy to be properly indignant.

'Well,' Krishna said, 'when we first came, he was always making me wash. All over at night and my hands before meals. Now he does not say anything about washing, and I like that better.'

Mary giggled until her stomach shook. 'I expect the habit's just worn off,' she said. 'At home, you see, he's always doing things like that—teaching Polly-Anna proper manners and making them change their socks and clean their teeth.'

'In my family,' Krishna said, 'men do not look after children.'

'Things are different in England,' Mary said. 'And though Simon's mother is nice, she's sort of vague, and she doesn't bother much. Simon doesn't have to, either—I mean, no one makes him, and if I was him I wouldn't.'

'Nor would I,' Krishna said.

They turned their heads and grinned at each other.

'Pull some faces, Mary,' Krishna said.

'I'm too tired.'

'Tell me a story, then. Tell me some more about your Horrible Aunt.'

'I've told you it all.' Mary felt uncomfortable suddenly. She raised her head to see if Simon was anywhere around. He wasn't, but the uncomfortable feeling remained. She said crossly, 'Why do you keep on and on?'

'I like stories,' Krishna said. 'What will happen if she finds out what you are doing? Being with us, on the island?'

Mary pretended not to hear. She stared up at the sky.

Krishna shifted closer, leaning on his elbow so he could look into her face.

'Will it be something dreadful?' he said. 'Will she cut off your hands and feet?'

Mary was shocked. She saw his eyes, shining like lamps.

She said, in her sternest voice, 'Of course not. I expect she'd just shut me in my room and feed me on bread and water.'

She could tell by his disappointed expression that this was not nearly horrid enough for him, and sighed inwardly. She wished she had never begun on this silly story about Aunt Alice —and not just because she was bored with telling it. It struck her that telling lies was really rather a lot of trouble! Once you started, you had to go on and on. It was like pouring water into a hole in the sand; there was never any end to it, never any finish . . .

'Tell me about the time she tried to poison you,' Krishna said. 'About the blue bottle marked Poison, and how you found it and poured the poison away and filled it up with water.'

Mary said quickly, 'You didn't tell Simon that did you?'

Krishna had promised, but you never knew!

'I said I would not,' Krishna said. 'Besides, he would not believe me. Simon likes things to be true, always.'

Mary looked at him. She wasn't sure what he meant— whether Simon wouldn't believe some of the more far-fetched things she had told Krishna, or whether Krishna himself didn't.

Krishna said, 'I mean, he would believe about your Aunt being cruel, but not about the poison.'

Mary sat up. She realised that it would be perfectly easy to say, 'But none of it is true, none of it at all,'—and later on she was to wish she had said that—but then the tin can rattled over and she forgot all about it, in the excitement of landing a fish.

Krishna untied the line from his ankle and began to pull it

in, making his way down the bluff to a small beach. He brought in a brown trout that flapped and wriggled on the gravel.

'Too small,' Mary said. She unhooked it carefully and threw it back in the lake. Krishna, who was squeamish, turned his back.

'It's all right,' Mary said. 'You can look now. Though if you like fishing, you ought to be able to do this part of it, too.'

But she felt relieved herself. She hated it, when the trout was big enough to kill.

'It was under eight inches,' she said to Simon, who had appeared at the top of the bluff.

He nodded, squatted on the bank, and fitted a fresh lot of worms on the hook. 'Not much chance of a big one, really,' he said as he threw the line out. 'Sun's getting round to this part of the lake.'

'Why eight inches?' Krishna asked.

'It's the law. If you eat all the little ones, they get no chance to grow big and breed.'

'I thought we were outlaws,' Krishna said. 'Outlaws do not take notice of the law.'

'Some laws make sense and some don't,' Simon said. 'And we're not outlaws, really. More refugees.' He replaced the tin can on the pile of stones.

'Me from the English police,' Krishna said, trying to see if he could hop one-legged up the steep bank. He collapsed halfway up and rolled down and lay on his back, grinning. A shaft of sun shone in his dark eyes and on his hair, which was shiny but dusty. Like blackberries at the side of a busy road, Mary thought. 'And Mary from her horrible Aunt,' Krishna said.

Mary glanced at Simon, who was fastening the heavy line

round the tin, and then on to a tree root that stuck out of the bank. She had the feeling that he was deliberately not looking at her.

She said, to change the subject, 'What about Noakes? What's Noakes a refugee from?'

Simon said, 'Noakes? Oh, Noakes is a refugee from civilisation. He's the biggest refugee of us all.'

After the first few days they had hardly seen him. He had gone wild. Now he came sometimes, when they were cooking fish, and crouched, waiting for his share, but mostly they only saw him at a distance: a flash of fur in the undergrowth. Once, when Simon had got up in the night, he had seen him playing on the bluff in the moonlight; a lolloping creature, a black shadow, dancing on three legs and growling and playing with his own tail, like a kitten. In the daytime he was often near, but liked, it seemed, to remain unseen; stalking them through the rhododendrons and the brambles, and lying still, belly to earth, whenever they came close to him. His bandage had fallen off and he had grown fat and glossy. He caught his own food: field mice and birds that he scrunched up delicately, leaving only feathers, and once Mary had found him with a small rabbit. He had snarled at her menacingly, glaring with his one eye, and she had backed away.

She was afraid that one day he would disappear altogether, but Simon said he would stay.

'He can't get away, actually,' he said. 'Not unless he learns to swim. I mean, there's only one way, across the bridge, and I don't suppose he can balance on the beam, not with only three legs. He'll never leave the island.'

'Nor am I going to,' Krishna said. 'Never.'

'Never is a long time,' Simon said.

'Not too long for me. I shall stay until I am an old, old man.'

'In this book I read,' Simon said, 'the people who built the grotto hired a man to live here and pretend to be a hermit. They thought it would be romantic to have a real live hermit living in their grotto to show their friends when they brought them on picnics, and they paid him two hundred pounds to wear ragged clothes and sit and think, but he got fed up after a while and went away.'

'He must have been mad,' Krishna said.

'Oh, I dunno. I expect he just got bored, being on his own.'

'I would never be bored,' Krishna said. 'I shall stay here and be a hermit, Simon, when you go back to school.'

'Don't use dirty words,' Simon said, and groaned.

Krishna giggled. 'Don't you like school, Simon?'

Mary said quickly, 'No one does, in their right mind.' She thought this was an unfortunate subject to have got on to. Simon was looking thoughtful, which was a bad sign. He had never said how long he could stay on the island, away from home, and she hadn't asked him. She didn't want him to start thinking about it now.

She said, 'Do you know, the nuts are ripe? I looked this morning. The cob tree, by the rowan.'

They knew which tree she meant. They knew every tree, every bush. The island was perhaps half a mile long and a quarter wide; the boys never left it, and every morning when she came, balancing easily on the bridge beam now, Mary felt as if she were entering a fortress, a castle. The lake was the moat round it and the grotto its inner keep, its sanctum. Some-times they built a fire in the centre chamber and watched the flames change the colour of the crystal roof.

It was damp there, because the lake ran through it, but the inner room where Simon and Krishna slept, was warm and dry. They had covered the floor with dried, crinkly bracken that smelt sweet and musty.

Mary envied them this heavenly bed. Sheets seemed so dull—as indeed, everything seemed so dull now, off the island. Leaving it at night and going home, was like stepping into a black and white film, after colour . . .

'I'm afraid you're having rather a boring time, Mary,' Grandfather said. 'My fault. I'm sorry.'

He had rheumatism in his knees and couldn't swim. 'Typical,' he grumbled, 'absolutely typical. Best summer for years, and here I am, laid up!'

'You'd only get heat stroke on the beach,' Aunt Alice said. 'Filthy, too. All that oil.'

'It's nicer inland,' Mary said. 'In the woods.'

'Which woods?' Grandfather looked at her frowning.

'Oh—just woods.'

'Not the same as the beach, though. What d'you find to do? With that chum of yours—what's his name? Trumper?'

'Trumpet,' Aunt Alice said.

'Nothing much,' Mary said. 'Just messing about.'

'You must do something. Day after day. Out of the house as soon as breakfast is over, not back till supper. Can't *just mess about* all that time!'

Mary wished her grandfather would stop asking questions. He didn't usually pry, but the pain in his legs made him fretful.

'There's nuts to pick,' she said. 'And blackberries . . .'

Even if she could tell him the truth, it would be hard to explain what they did. Every day was the same, and yet marvellously different . . .

'Leave her alone, Father,' Aunt Alice said. 'Messing about's a good occupation, for someone her age. I used to like the woods, too. More than the beach . . . '

She smiled at Mary, as if they shared a secret.

'All right,' Grandfather said. 'All right, Alice. I'm a crochety old man. A crochety, tetchy, curmudgeonly old man with creaky knees. Don't get old, Mary.'

Mary shook her head. It seemed easy advice to take. She felt quite sure at this moment that she would never change from the person she was now, and that things would go on as they were, for ever and ever . . .

They had picked all the blackberries on the island. 'There's some good ones at the side of the path coming down,' Mary said. 'Before you get to the lake. By the fallen tree. They're a bit high up, but we could reach them with sticks.'

Simon shook his head. 'I want those for my Mum. I always pick her a good lot for jam, before I go back to school.'

'Who's using dirty words now?' Mary said.

'Look at this leaf,' Krishna said. It was browny-red and crisp, like a cornflake.

'Autumn,' Simon said. 'Witless loon. Leaves change colour and fall in the autumn.'

'Witless loon yourself,' Krishna said, and punched him in the stomach. 'We don't have autumn in Africa.'

'Tins are running low,' Simon said. 'No more baked beans. No more peaches. No more tomato soup.'

'Peach tins are heavy,' Mary said. 'But I can get beans. And soup.'

'We want more line, too. I put out an eel line last night across the culvert, but it rained and it got washed away.'

'It didn't rain last night,' Mary said.

'It did, you know. Everywhere was soaked this morning.'

'Just dew. *It didn't rain.*'

Simon looked at her stubborn mouth. 'All right, have it your own way. All the same, we need new line, and some tins, and Krishna ought to have another jersey. He's torn that old one of yours to shreds and it gets a bit nippy now, evenings.'

'I can get him another,' Mary said. 'And some vests too, if he's cold. I've got hundreds of lovely, thick, woolly vests. And I can get the tins and the line. I can get anything you like . . .'

She stood in the queue at the Post Office, fretting. It was five o'clock and the shops closed at half past. Everyone in front of her seemed very slow and old; old men buying postal orders and stamps, and old women drawing their pensions. They took ages, taking their money, counting change with stiff slow fingers, putting notes away in one part of their purses, coins in another. Some of them lingered for a nice little chat with the clerk behind the counter, and some of them had dogs on leads that got tangled up with other people's legs.

The woman behind Mary said, 'Goodness, what a time! Patience on a monument!'

She had a pointed, witch-like face. *Simon's Gran.* For a moment, Mary's heart bumped—absurdly, of course, because there was nothing to be afraid of. Or so she thought . . .

'How are you, dear?'

'Very well, thank you,' Mary said, and added, cunningly, 'How's Simon? I haven't seen him for *ages.*'

'Away camping. He likes to get off on his own for a bit, and I can't say I blame him!' Simon's Gran smiled, and her face was all lines, like a nut. 'That family! Monkey house at the Zoo!'

Mary had reached the counter now. She had two pounds and fourpence in her Post Office book, and she drew it all out except for a shilling. She turned to say goodbye to Simon's Gran—and saw that someone had joined her.

'Your turn, Mother,' Mrs Carver said to Simon's Gran, and then, to Mary, 'Well, you're quite a stranger! Always gone now, time I get to your Auntie's in the morning!'

Mary stared. Mrs Carver's hair was red and her mother's grizzled black and white like a shaving brush, but otherwise, seeing them together, the likeness was unmistakable. Two pale, sharp faces . . .

Mary caught her breath. She had thought Simon's mother had reminded her of someone! Now she knew who it was. She and Mrs Carver were sisters. Mrs Trumpet's hair was dark like her mother's, like the twins. But Simon had red hair, though it wasn't as bright as Mrs Carver's. More gingery . . .

'. . . having a lovely time, your Auntie tells me,' Mrs Carver was saying.

Mary nodded. Her stomach was screwed up. What else had Aunt Alice said? *She's found a friend, a boy called Simon Trumpet?* She had told Simon's Gran, she hadn't seen him for ages . . .

Mrs Carver said, 'I must say I'm glad to hear it. You know, your poor Auntie was quite worried about you, mooning about on your own. It's not natural, Mrs Carver, she said to me, a child should have other children to play with.'

Mary fidgeted. 'Yes. Well. I've got to go now . . .' She gave Simon's Gran one last, forced smile, and darted for the door.

Two small, solid figures barred her way, both wailing like fire sirens.

'Gran. GRAN. I dropped me lolly.'

'So she pinched *mine*.' Poll stamped her foot. 'Gran, tell her. It's NOT FAIR.'

'It is. You *joggled* me.'

'Not a-purpose.'

'You did.'

'Didn't.'

'Liar. PIG LIAR.'

They fell upon each other in the doorway. Mrs Carver pushed past Mary and separated them.

'What a noise! I'm ashamed of the pair of you.'

'I want GRAN.' Poll pushed Mrs Carver's hands away and opened her mouth to scream—long, high, piercing screams, like a train whistling.

'Gran's getting her pension,' Mrs Carver said, and slapped Poll on her fat, bare leg. 'Move out of the way now, how d'you think people can get by?'

'S'not *people*,' Annabel said. 'It's Mary. Poll, look, it's *Mary*.'

Poll's screams stopped, as if someone had turned a switch. Two dear little faces were lifted, four bright eyes, two red, button noses.

'Hallo,' Mary said, gloomily.

'I didn't know you knew Mary,' Mrs Carver said, dabbing away busily at their tear-streaked faces. The twins jerked their heads up and down, like ponies.

' 'Course we know Mary, Auntie.'

'She came to *lunch*. Just once, though. She didn't come again.'

'I'm not surprised,' Mrs Carver said, giving a final, twisting wipe to Poll's nose, and standing back to survey the result of her efforts.

'She was hungry,' Poll said indignantly. 'She was *jolly glad* to come and have lunch with us.'

'Hungry?' Mrs Carver looked curiously at Mary, who wished the earth would open beneath her.

'She's a Norphan,' Poll said.

'A poor Orphan,' Annabel said, in an oozy, sentimental voice. 'She's got a strict Auntie, who doesn't give her enough to eat.'

'Really?' Mrs Carver looked at Mary. Her mouth twitched, and there was a bright, sardonic gleam in her eye.

Mary thought of flinging herself to the ground in a fit. Or killing herself. Instead, she ran: out of the Post Office and along the High Street, head down, blundering into people . . .

She felt she would never stop running. That if she did, something awful would catch up with her . . .

ELEVEN

'Chip-chop weather change . . .'

MARY PACKED A jersey for Krishna, and two of the thick
woollen vests Aunt Alice had bought her. She packed a spare
pair of jeans for herself, extra socks and shoes, her anorak and
her hairbrush. She went down to the kitchen, stepping carefully over the stair that squeaked and took some cheese and
bread from the larder. Then she went into the garden to put
the bag in the bushes by the gate, ready for leaving.

It was so early that mist lay on the ground in curls, but she
had already been up for hours, sitting on the edge of her bed
with a hollow feeling inside her.

It came from sadness, not hunger, but now, standing in the
cold, pearly grass, she decided that food might help. She went
back into the house, into the kitchen; ate four thick slices of
bread and raspberry jam, and put the kettle on the stove. The
boiler in the kitchen murmured and sang; she warmed her
cold hands on the pipe above it, and sucked the raspberry pips
out of her teeth.

The hollowness in her stomach persisted. She stared at the
faces that seemed to rise up in front of her, and listened to voices
in her mind.

Mrs Carver's face, sharp and pointed; Aunt Alice's, rabbity
and pale. Mrs Carver saying, *Well, that's what she told them, true as
I stand here, the wicked girl! An orphan, living with a cruel Aunt . . .*

And Aunt Alice's face, turning a piteous, slow red . . .

Mary moaned softly and leaned her forehead against the pipe until it began to burn her.

She thought—Perhaps it won't happen like that, after all! But what could prevent it? Only Mrs Carver dying suddenly in the night. Or being run over on the way to work this morning.

She was the sort of woman who would feel it her duty to tell Aunt Alice what her niece had been saying about her, behind her back.

And Aunt Alice would believe that Mary hated her . . .

The kettle began to sing and Mary looked at the kitchen clock. It was nearly seven-thirty, and Mrs Carver would be here by nine.

She laid a tray and warmed the pot and made the tea, good and strong the way Aunt Alice liked it, but never made it for herself. She said it was a waste to make a pot for one person, and that strong tea was bad for Grandfather's heart.

As she carried the tray upstairs, she thought the house seemed curiously dark. She looked out of the landing window. There was no sign of the mist lifting.

Aunt Alice struggled up in bed, fumbling a woollen bed jacket over her shoulders. She wore a hairnet, and her two front teeth reposed on a grinning, pink bridge in the glass on the table beside her. After one glance, Mary looked politely away. She said, 'I just thought you'd like some tea, Aunt Alice.'

'Oh,' Aunt Alice said. 'Oh! Mary *dear* . . .'

She blinked her eyes rapidly and gasped. She seemed overwhelmed—as if, Mary thought, suddenly wanting to giggle, she had been presented with a cheque for a thousand pounds, instead of a pot of tea!

'I hope I made it right,' Mary said. 'I put in five shovels.'

Aunt Alice poured a cup. It looked quite black.

'Just right,' Aunt Alice said. 'Perfect! Tea in bed! What luxury! I feel like the Queen of England.'

Mary stood at the end of the bed. She wanted to go and she wanted to stay.

Aunt Alice looked at the window. 'Where's the old sun this morning? Chip-chop, weather change ...'

Mary shifted from one foot to the other.

'Oh well, I suppose it couldn't last for ever. All good things come to an end,' Aunt Alice said, smiling at Mary.

Mary wished there was something she could say to Aunt Alice, but there was nothing except *Goodbye* and she couldn't say that. So she just smiled, awkwardly and shyly, and walked backwards to the door.

Outside, she stood still for a minute. Her eyes had misted over. Now she had taken the tea, there was nothing else she could think of to make Aunt Alice feel better.

Apart from leaving the note.

She pulled it out of her pocket now, and went into her bedroom to prop it up on the dressing table, where Aunt Alice would see it as soon as she opened the door.

Dear Aunt Alice,

I am sorry to go without telling you, but you won't want me to stay any longer, now you know what I've done.

Yours sincerely,

Mary.

P.S. Give Grampy my love and say thank you for having me.

P.P.S. It was all lies I told.

She had written the letter last night, and had spent a long time trying to think of the right thing to say. Now, reading it

again, water came into her eyes and nose. She sniffed and
pressed her knuckles into her eyes until coloured arrows shot
across the blackness. She thought that in a way it would be
comforting to be a crying sort of person; to lie down on her
bed and howl.

Instead, she blew her nose, looked round the room, and left
it, shutting the door softly behind her.

'I've run away,' she said to Simon.

He didn't answer. He was standing on his head against the
wall of the grotto and counting. 'Hundred and sixty eight,
hundred and sixty nine, hundred and seventy ...'

'Simon.'

'Hundred and seventy three, hundred and seventy four ...'

'Simon, *listen* ...'

He swung right side up, red-faced and annoyed.

'You've broken my concentration,' he accused her. 'It's no
good now. You've got to keep it up to five hundred or it
doesn't work.'

'What doesn't work?'

'Yogi. For blushing and stammering. I sent off for a book.
You have to learn to concentrate your mind. It's a matter of
the way you breathe. Standing on your head and counting is
the first exercise. What d'you mean, you've run away?'

She said, scornfully, 'You weren't concentrating very hard,
were you? Not if you heard what I said.'

'Oh shut up.' He turned away, kicking a stone. The back of
his neck had flushed scarlet. He picked up the stone, walked
to the mouth of the grotto, and skimmed it across the lake. It
hopped seven times, startling a moor hen that streaked across
the water, red legs trailing. Simon said, 'D'you mean you're
staying here, then?'

'Yes.'

'Why? I mean, what made you change your mind?'

Her throat seemed to have dried up. She sucked saliva out of her cheeks and swallowed.

'I found out something last night. Your Aunt works for my Aunt. Cleaning.'

'I know. It's a small world.' Simon skimmed another stone, but it only hopped twice. 'Damn,' he said.

'You *what?*'

'I said, I know. Why don't you wash your ears sometimes?' *His* ears were crimson. He said, affectedly casual, 'Evening before we came here, she was round at our house and she mentioned your Auntie had a niece staying. Name of Mary. Eleven, going on twelve. So I asked questions. Not too many, just to make sure.'

'I bet I know the sort of things she said about me.'

'Well.' Simon began to grin. Then he caught Mary's eye. She said furiously, 'Why didn't you tell me?'

'Oh, it seemed best left.' He scrabbled up handfuls of stones and gravel and threw them in the lake. 'One thing—you might have thought I was trying to catch you out.'

'Oh,' Mary said, terribly humiliated. 'Oh. Yes. I see.'

'I *wasn't*, you know,' Simon said. 'It was pure chance. And I didn't tell her I knew you.'

'She knows now. I met her at the post office with Polly-Anna. It was awful.'

The memory of how awful it had been swept over her like a wave: she felt as if she were drowning beneath it. She sat against the grotto wall and put her head in her hands. Tears spurted through her fingers. 'They told her about me being an orphan and starving and she'll tell my Aunt Alice . . . and . . . and . . . oh, *I wish I was dead.*'

She heard the crunch of Simon's feet. Then nothing except the sound of the water in the grotto. He had gone away and left her alone.

She went on crying. Once she had started, it seemed impossible to stop. It was as if a dam had burst inside her and would go on, pouring out water through her eyes and nose until she was dried out and empty. Her hands were clammy, like soaking sponges, and her head had swollen to twice its size.

Simon said, 'Mary.' He was trying to pull her hands from her face. She twisted away, bubbling out words like tears.

'Leave me alone.'

He was trying to push something into the narrow space between her knees and her schest. Something wriggling and furry.

'*Noakes*.' She clasped him, burying her face in his coat. He resisted her stiffly, clawing her legs, and she had to let him go. He sprang from her lap and sat a few feet away, cleaning his ruffled coat and watching her.

'Everyone hates me. Even Noakes,' Mary said.

'It's only because I grabbed him,' Simon said. 'He doesn't like being grabbed at, you know.' He waited a minute. 'Shall I go away?'

'Yes,' Mary said, and chewed at her lip. 'I mean, no. No.'

He squatted beside her, frowning. Neither of them spoke, and after a little, Noakes came up of his own accord and rubbed against Mary's leg.

She didn't touch him, just let him rub and purr.

'You're the only one he'll do that to,' Simon said. 'Please cheer up, Mary.'

'I am cheered up. I just feel jellified. Rubbery and flabby. Like an empty hot water bottle.'

'That's crying,' Simon said. 'It leaves you like that.'

'I don't often cry. In fact I never do, usually.'

'Nothing to be proud of, not crying. Everyone cries!' Simon chucked a stone at the opposite wall of the grotto. It tinkled on the crystals and plopped into the lake. 'Why d'you have to be different from other people?'

'I don't want *them* to see I'm unhappy. Crying gives you away.'

'Them?'

She didn't answer.

'D'you mean your Aunt and your grandfather?'

She shook her head. Her stomach seemed tied in knots. She burst out, 'If *your* parents were always going off, would you want the rotten things to see you minded?'

'*Do* you mind?' He blushed. 'I'm sorry. My Aunt told me. But it's none of my business.'

'It's all right.' She thought for a minute. 'No, I don't mind,' she said, surprised. 'I did, but I don't now. Not anymore.'

She felt peaceful, suddenly, as if the knots in her stomach had loosened.

She said, 'It's different now. I don't know why. Since Krishna, and coming to the island. Where's he gone? I haven't seen him this morning.'

'Nutting,' Simon said. 'Thinks of nothing but his inside, that boy.'

He hadn't picked many nuts, though. One small billy can. He was sitting beside it, knees drawn up to his chest.

'I feel sick,' he said.

He looked sick. Not pale, of course, because of his skin, but dingy.

'Too many sardines last night,' Simon said. 'I told you.'

'I'm cold,' Krishna said.

'You can't be. Weather's changed a bit, but not *cold*. Just no sun. You want to run about.'

'I've got a pain.'

He looked small and young and miserable. Mary knelt beside him. 'I've brought you a jersey, and some lovely woolly vests. Put them on and you'll feel better.'

But even with the vest on, buttoned to the neck, and a thick jersey on top, he was still shivery.

It seemed absurd, because although the sun didn't come out, the day grew noticeably hotter. The sky was dark, woolly grey, pressing down like a soft ceiling on the tops of the trees and seeming to cut off, not only sun, but sound. No birds sang, and once, when a duck took off from the lake, the clapping of its wings was so loud it made them jump. The bird left a spreading wake, but as soon as that had gone, the lake was still again, brown and opaque, reflecting nothing. Even the air seemed different: the sweat formed on their foreheads and the air didn't dry them. It was so heavy with moisture, so damp and thick, that it seemed as if it could be scooped up in a ladle.

No one wanted much lunch. It was too much effort. Mary and Simon managed a mouthful or two, but Krishna ate nothing. He lay curled up, and seemed to be dozing.

'Over-excitement last night,' Simon said. 'Sardines, and then I thought I heard a vixen. So I took him to look—he's never seen a fox, and I thought it would be interesting.'

'Did you find it?'

'No. We saw Noakes hunting though. Crouching, and wriggling his bottom, and then—phwoooot! *Charge*. We didn't see, but we heard something cry. I don't think Krishna liked that. He doesn't like things being killed. It kept him awake.'

'I feel *hot* now,' Krishna complained.

Simon got up. 'Best thing you can do is go into the grotto and have your sleep out.' He put his hand on Krishna's forehead and looked startled. Then he said, ' 'Course you feel hot! What d'you expect if you put all those clothes on, a day like this! Vests and jerseys—as if this was the Arctic Circle, or something. You must be raving!'

He spoke in the bothered, grown-up voice Mary had not heard him use for a long time. She wondered if he was worried, but if he was, he didn't say so. He took Krishna to the grotto and came back, mopping his forehead, and said the best thing *they* could do, was get in the lake.

It was warm, like bathwater. Too inert to swim, they lay on their backs, paddling idly with their hands, and let an unseen current carry them slowly into the middle of the lake. Mary's hair floated over her face like seaweed, tickling her mouth, but she felt too lazy to brush it away. She rolled over instead, like a turning log, and opened her eyes under water. Sometimes, on a sunny day, she had seen great clumps of weed, a swaying, watery forest with fish swimming through the branches instead of birds, and once she had seen nine big trout—she had counted them exactly—lying in a little hollow at the bottom of the lake, so still that she had thought it would be quite easy to catch them, until she tried . . . But today she could see nothing, only a thick, brown murkiness, as if someone had taken a giant spoon and stirred up all the sludge from the bottom of the water, turning it into soup. Mary swam face downwards, holding her breath, until her hands touched the carpet of curly weed that covered part of the lake. Then she lifted her head, gasping, and looked for Simon.

He was nowhere to be seen. The sky was almost quite black now, and it was so dark . . . Not only couldn't she see Simon, she couldn't see the shore . . .

Then the first lightning came; not a zigzag flicker, but a still, almost blinding illumination, as if a light had suddenly been switched on. She saw Simon's head like a seal's, poking up.

She called, 'Simon,' and the thunder answered her—a crash, as if the earth were being torn apart. She swam towards him in darkness, but only for a second: there was another flash of lightning that seemed to strike down into the water. She saw weeds twisting and writhing beneath her like trees tossed in a violent storm, although on the surface no wind ruffled the water, and the rhododendron bushes on the island, white when the lighning flashed, were still as carved stone.

Simon shouted something. She thought he said, *Fine old storm*, but the words were drowned by thunder that rolled and crashed, and then by the rain: white, steel rods hammering on the water as if on solid glass. It was like swimming through a waterfall. As she reached Simon, something struck her cheek and made her gasp. 'Hail,' he said, and she saw it plopping all round her: ice bullets, making neat, round holes in the lake.

They swam into the grotto, their knees grinding on gravel. They dragged themselves onto the floor of the cavern, too spent at first to do more than lie there, looking at the storm. In the lightning, the hail was like a curtain of diamonds falling.

Simon said, 'My Uncle Horace had his car struck by lightning once. He said everything went blue, and smelt of seaweed.'

'Seaweed?' Mary said. She began to shiver and Simon threw her his shirt. 'Dry on that,' he said, but the shirt was damp, as if it had been hanging in steam. When they were dressed, they felt almost as wet as they had been in the lake. 'Ought to jump up and down,' Simon said, but after one or two half-hearted bending and stretching exercises, they gave up and huddled together, watching the lightning bounce like a skimmed pebble across the lake, and waiting for each cannonade of thunder. These were so frequent now, and so tearingly loud, that it seemed impossible to hear themselves speak, let alone any other sound. When one came, a long, unearthly scream, they stood for the moment, rigid and appalled ...

Then Simon shouted, '*Krishna*,' and leapt for the rocky stair.

But it was Noakes who had made that terrible noise. Lightning lit the tiny room and they saw Krishna, lying on the bracken, the sleeping bag pulled over his head, while Noakes stalked the room like a mad tiger, tail erect, fur bristling, one eye blazing. When Mary bent to touch him, he arched away, gave another blood-curdling cry, and bounded past her.

Simon caught her arm. 'Let him go, he'll scratch you to pieces,' he shouted. 'He's fighting wild ...'

Thunder crackled, like something solid breaking. When it died away, echoes grumbling through the grotto, they heard Noakes's high-pitched yowl, growing fainter as he went further away.

And closer, in the room, Krishna weeping ...

They knelt beside him. Simon pulled off the sleeping bag and Mary took him in her arms, cradling his head and crooning. 'It's all right ... all right ... only a silly old storm ...'

But he continued to cry, twisting in the bracken and jerking his knees up to his chest. His forehead, pressed against Mary's chest, felt burning hot.

She said, 'Simon, it's not the storm. He's ill. He's hot as fire. Krishna. Darling. Where do you hurt?'

The boy moaned something. Mary didn't catch it.

'I think his stomach,' Simon said. He felt Krishna gently. 'It's funny. Feel . . .'

Below Krishna's ribs, his belly pushed out, hard and tight as a football. He cried out when Mary touched him.

'Perhaps he ate something bad,' Simon said. 'Berries. Perhaps he just needs to be sick. If we make him put a finger down his throat . . . or tickle it with a piece of bracken . . .'

'Revolting,' Mary said, and pulled a face.

'It's not a time to be fussy. We got to do something.'

Lightning frayed the room. A feebler flash than before, but it showed Simon's face, chalk-white. 'Do you want him to *die?*'

The word echoed, fading away through the caves and passages of the grotto like the next thunder clap which sounded so gently that it was more like an enormous sigh. As if the whole earth had suddenly grown tired.

'Storm's moving away,' Simon said, glancing upwards. As he spoke, a faint light began to filter into the room through the small window. The ordinary light of day.

'I will die,' Krishna said suddenly, and gave a choking gasp of terror. 'I will die.'

'Of course not,' Mary said, holding him close and glaring nastily at Simon. 'Don't take any notice of *him*.'

'I hurt,' Krishna wailed. 'Mary. Oh, please. Make it stop.'

He rolled on to his side and buried his head in her lap. She cupped her hands over his ears and looked at Simon.

'Get Aunt Alice,' she said. 'She used to be a nurse. She'll know what to do.'

TWELVE

After the Storm

MARY NURSED KRISHNA and sang to him. Whenever he moaned, she felt his pain, like a stab in her own stomach. And also fear . . .

In between the songs, she questioned him anxiously. 'Is it better? Just a little bit? Do you feel better now?' until he said, 'Oh do stop, Mary. You can't make me better by *asking*.'

She was so relieved, she laughed and hugged him. If he had the energy to sound so cross, he couldn't be going to die!

She went on singing until her voice was croaky and he grew heavier in her arms. When she was sure he was fast asleep, she made him comfortable in the bracken and left the grotto.

The storm had blown itself out and left a fine, windy evening: silver ripples on the lake and bright-edged rags of cloud scudding across a greenish sky. On her way to the bridge she called Noakes once or twice, but there was no sign of him.

Nor of Simon. She sat in the middle of a rhododendron bush where she could watch the bridge without being seen. Her arms ached from holding Krishna, and her heart ached, too. Now the waiting was nearly over she was afraid—not for Krishna, anymore, but for herself. Aunt Alice would come and rescue Krishna, but there would be no rescue for her! She had been a traitor, and by now Aunt Alice would know it! The thought made Mary shudder and hunch into herself. She couldn't face Aunt Alice. She couldn't . . .

'I can't,' Aunt Alice said. 'I can't . . .'
She stood on the first half of the bridge, looking with horror at the narrow beam. She wore a shapeless raincoat that reached almost to her ankles, and her grey hair, blown loose from its bun, fanned round her face like witch's locks. Mary thought she looked beautiful.
'It's all right,' Simon said. 'Long as you don't look.'
'Well,' Aunt Alice said. 'I don't know . . . '
'I'll blindfold you,' Simon offered. He pulled a grubby handkerchief out of his pocket.
Aunt Alice stood still while he fastened it. The tied ends stood up above her head like rabbit's ears. Pale as a turnip, she took her first, teetering step on the beam.
'Oh,' she said. 'Oh, my goodness!'
'I'm holding you,' Simon said. 'All you got to do is put one foot in front of the other. Feel with your toes.'
Aunt Alice lifted her feet high, like a bird stepping through water.
'You're doing fine,' Simon said.
He moved cautiously backwards, clasping Aunt Alice's hands. They looked very funny, but Mary didn't smile.
'We should have waited for the boat,' Aunt Alice said, and halted suddenly.
'This is quicker.'
Aunt Alice gasped. 'Not if we fall off.'
'You won't fall if you keep moving,' Simon said.
Step by shaky step. From time to time, Aunt Alice made small, squeaky sounds of terror. Mary shut her eyes.
'*There*,' Simon said, at last. 'It's not far to the grotto now.'

'I think I remember,' Aunt Alice said.

Mary wondered what she meant. They passed by her bush, so close that she could have put out her hand and touched Aunt Alice's raincoat.

When she judged they had reached the grotto, she followed them, creeping a little way up the twisting stair. She heard Aunt Alice say, 'Oh the poor child, the poor baby,' and Krishna's answering murmur.

'Been asleep, have you?' Aunt Alice said. 'Well, that's the best thing. Where does it hurt you, my love?'

Her voice was so kind. Mary thought—She never spoke to *me* like that, and rubbed the back of her hand, deliberately, against the spiky crystals on the wall. Then she sucked the blood from the scratches and sighed. Aunt Alice would have done, if only she'd let her. And now it was too late . . .

'All right, darling,' Aunt Alice was saying. 'I won't touch your poor tummy again. Yes I know it hurts, my pet, but we're going to make it better, quite soon. A nice man is coming in a boat and we're going to take you to a nice, warm hospital. Simon—go and see if your Uncle's coming . . .'

Mary ran, jumping the narrow neck of the lake to the other side of the grotto and hiding in a tiny room that had a small, slotted window. She could see a small segment of the central cavern.

She heard Simon call, 'Uncle Horace, we're here,' and then an answering hail from the lake. The boat glided in, rowlocks creaking as the rower shipped his oars.

Simon said, 'She's bringing him down.'

'And you standing there?' Uncle Horace said. 'Letting a lady . . .'

'It's all right, Mr Trumpet. He weighs nothing. No more than a bird, the poor lamb.'

Standing on tiptoe, Mary could see Aunt Alice's face as she appeared down the rocky stairs, and Krishna's head, resting against her shoulder.

Simon giggled. 'I should've thought a lamb weighed a bit more than a bird.'

'Enough cheek from you,' Aunt Alice said calmly. 'Get in the boat. I'll put him on your lap.'

She vanished from Mary's view. The boat creaked.

'There's a boyo,' Uncle Horace's voice boomed hollow in the grotto. 'Soon have you tucked up in bed.'

Mary stood with her face to the wall. In a minute they would be gone, all of them. And Aunt Alice hadn't once mentioned her name . . .

The splash of oars, and voices, growing fainter. Then nothing. Silence. She was alone. They had gone and left her alone. Although this was what she had wanted—to be left on the island, an outcast, an outlaw—tears pricked the back of her eyes.

Aunt Alice said, 'Mary . . .'

She peeped through the slit. Aunt Alice was still standing there.

'Mary. Where are you, dear?'

Mary held her breath.

Aunt Alice said in a loud, conversational voice, 'I think it may be his appendix. Poor little chap. Mr Trumpet will take him to the hospital in his van. Simon rang him at the shop and he came straight round.'

She stopped and waited. Listening. She said, 'Mary . . .'

Mary didn't move.

Aunt Alice said, 'You know, I used to come here myself when I was about your age. The bridge wasn't so broken down then, but no one else came. I used to come on my bike and leave it by the old gate. The path's overgrown a bit since. I don't remember all those nettles! I remember how I felt, though. Coming here by myself, I could be someone quite different. Pretty and clever. I used to pretend my parents weren't my real parents, that they had only adopted me. I was really a Duke's daughter. I expect it sounds silly.'

She paused—hopefully, it seemed. Mary felt an itch in her nose. She pressed her finger on her upper lip, to stop herself sneezing.

Aunt Alice said, 'I even told people sometimes. Strangers, of course. Then I was terrified my parents would find out. I used to have nightmares . . .' She laughed her high, nervous laugh, and turned it into a cough. 'If you're not coming, dear, I'll have to go back on my own. Although I'm not sure how I'll manage the bridge.'

Mary had managed to stop the sneeze. She let out her breath, very gently.

Aunt Alice turned and left the grotto. Small stones rattled as she climbed up the side of the bluff.

Mary followed, keeping her distance. Brambles plucked at her clothes. Aunt Alice didn't look back.

Mary thought—Perhaps she'll fall off the bridge! If she did, she would leap in, and save her! She would drag her to the bank and then sink back, exhausted, and let the quick-mud drag her down. She would die, saving Aunt Alice from death . . .

Ahead of her, Aunt Alice gave a sudden scream, and Mary's heart leapt. But there was no splash; Aunt Alice was nowhere near the bridge. It was Noakes that had frightened her, Mary saw as she ran forward; pouncing in front of her, his back arched, his fur on end. He looked fearsome . . .

'It's all right, Aunt Alice, it's only Noakes,' Mary shouted.

Aunt Alice turned, and Mary skidded to a stop beside her.

'Noakes?' Aunt Alice said.

'My cat.'

'Oh.' Aunt Alice looked at him. He was switching his tail and growling softly. Then he jumped sideways, into the undergrowth.

'He wouldn't have hurt you,' Mary said. 'He's just a bit nervous.'

'*Nervous?*'

'I mean, he's just not the sort of cat you can stroke.'

'It wouldn't occur to me to try,' Aunt Alice said.

Mary wondered what to say next. They couldn't go on talking about Noakes for ever!

Aunt Alice looked at her shyly, as if she were thinking the same thing.

Mary said, 'I can take you across the bridge, if you like.'

'Can you dear?' Aunt Alice's nose flushed pink and she stretched her jaw. 'I supposed we ought to be going, then. Mr Trumpet will be coming back to pick us up and take us to the hospital.'

It was very hot in the hospital and the lights were very bright. Aunt Alice and Uncle Horace went away with a starched and creaking nurse, and left their niece and nephew stranded in the waiting room, full of empty armchairs and tables covered with old magazines. Mary looked at one or two, but there was nothing interesting. She would have preferred to talk to Simon but he was very quiet and shut away: frightened or grumpy.

Once a group of nurses passed the door and looked in at them. They were whispering and giggling, and Mary heard one of them say, 'Are those the two kids, then?'

'They're talking about us,' she said. 'What cheek!'

Simon shrugged his shoulders. 'Might as well get used to it. I daresay it'll be all over the newspapers.'

This seemed unlikely, but exciting. 'Will it be on the telly, too?' Mary asked, but Simon only groaned and put his head in his hands.

They sat there for over an hour. When Aunt Alice and Uncle Horace came back, they were both half asleep in their chairs.

Uncle Horace said, 'Well, that's that. He's being operated on in about half an hour. They've managed to get hold of Mr Patel.'

Uncle Horace was a large man with a balding head and a grey beard that straggled unevenly, like an old floor mop. He had a large paunch with a stained red velvet waistcoat precariously fastened across it: as he bent to pick up his raincoat, one of the last buttons popped off.

Simon picked it up. His Uncle said, 'Well boyo, we'd better get on home and tell your Dad what you've been up to.'

Simon was very white.

Uncle Horace put a big hand on his shoulder. 'No point in putting things off,' he said.

'Simon's Dad's a policeman,' Mary whispered to Aunt Alice as they followed the others out of the hospital. She wondered if Simon was really frightened of his father, or if it was just his conscience worrying him again, now he had left the island.

She said, 'We *had* to hide Krishna, Aunt Alice. We just had to!'

'Oh, I can see,' Aunt Alice said. 'But other people may think differently, you must expect that.'

It was dark now, and had begun to rain. Heads down, they splashed through puddles on their way to the hospital car park.

Mary said, 'Is having your appendix out like tonsils?'

'Not so bad, in some ways. You don't get a sore throat. Don't worry, dear.'

'I'm not. I think Krishna's *lucky*.' Mary had enjoyed having her tonsils out: being in hospital and feeling important. 'Everyone being nice and bothering about him,' she said, and sighed.

Aunt Alice snatched Mary's hand, and tucked it under her arm.

Mary snuggled close. In the rainy cold, it was comforting. She said, 'What's going to happen, Aunt Alice?'

'Well.' Aunt Alice seemed to hesitate. 'I expect a policeman will want to see you. Just to ask a few questions. But you mustn't let that frighten you. I'll be there, or Grampy . . .'

'Oh, I shan't mind *that*. That'll be fabulously interesting.' Mary thought it was odd, the sort of thing grown-ups thought might frighten children! She said, 'But I didn't mean what'll happen to *me*. I meant, what'll happen to Krishna?'

'That'll be up to the Home Secretary,' Grandfather said. 'In the usual way children are not allowed to come and live here without their parents. Of course, it's possible that the Home Secretary may make an exception in Krishna's case, though I think it unlikely . . .'

'He jolly well better,' Mary said. 'After all we've done! I don't see what his parents have got to do with it, anyway. He's got his Uncle he can live with, hasn't he?'

'That's not the same thing as a mother or father, I'm afraid.'

'Uncles and Aunts are often much nicer,' Mary said.

Grandfather smiled, and lit his pipe. 'I meant, legally,' he said. 'As far as the law is concerned.' The smoke curled up round his shiny, baby's face as he went on, talking about dependent relatives, which were children and other people who couldn't earn their own living; and immigration laws and quotas. Although Mary was beginning to feel sleepy, after a hot bath and a huge supper, she tried to look as if she was wide awake and listening because Grandfather was so clearly enjoying himself explaining things to her, just as she had enjoyed herself earlier, telling him and Aunt Alice how she had rescued Krishna single-handed from the two men who had kidnapped him; and hidden him, and fed him . . .

'I thought the store cupboard was going down rather faster than usual!' Aunt Alice had said, but apart from this one remark, they had both listened without interruption and no mention of bedtime.

They were a much better audience than the policeman who had come while Mary was eating her supper. He had been very casual—almost *amused*, Mary had thought. He had asked her questions: about the date Krishna had arrived in England, and where they had hidden him, and why, and he had written her answers down in his notebook, but he had smiled a lot and made jokes, as if this was just a jolly game they were playing! Not a serious matter, at all!

Thinking about it now, made Mary angry. 'We *were* breaking the law, weren't we?' she said, interrupting her Grandfather's monologue.

He looked startled. 'Well, dear . . .' He tapped out his pipe. 'I know you didn't understand, but I suppose, strictly speaking . . .'

'Of course you were breaking the law, Mary,' Aunt Alice said. 'And rightly, to my mind!'

'Alice!' Grandfather said.

'Some laws are made to be broken,' Aunt Alice said.

'There's no point in sweeping things under the carpet! Pretending Mary and Simon didn't know what they were doing, and it was just a childish prank. It's—well—it's insulting to them both!'

She looked and sounded so indignant that Mary wished she could run and hug her.

'*Well* . . .' Grandfather said, and chuckled. Then he cleared his throat. 'Would it be insulting, Alice, to suggest she went to bed? It's late, and I suppose even hardened criminals get tired. And the next few days are likely to be rather exciting . . .' He filled his pipe again and spent rather a long time tamping the tobacco down. Then he looked at Aunt Alice over the flaring match and said, 'Have you told her yet?'

Aunt Alice said quickly, 'Come along, dear. Grampy's right. Time for Bedfordshire!'

Though this was the sort of silly remark that usually irritated Mary, it didn't tonight. It seemed just friendly, like someone putting an arm round your shoulders. She kissed her Grandfather and went upstairs, yawning and dragging her feet with Aunt Alice behind her, saying, 'Ups-i-daisy, now . . .'

It wasn't until she was in bed that she said, drowsily, 'Told me what? What haven't you told me?'

Aunt Alice was at the window. She drew the curtains back and stood for a minute, looking out. Then she came and sat on the edge of the bed and said, in a light, far-away voice, 'Your Mummy's coming in a few days' time.'

Mary said nothing. Round Aunt Alice's head, there was a fuzz of light from the lamp behind her. Mary narrowed her eyes and made the fuzz spiky.

'Won't that be nice?' Aunt Alice said.

Mary said, 'Yes,' because it was what Aunt Alice would expect her to say. She thought of asking if her mother was coming to take her home, and then of saying that she didn't want to go, but she knew she couldn't say that. Aunt Alice was being nice now, because she was a nice person, but underneath, deep down, she couldn't really want her to stay. Not after all the things Mary had said about her.

Mary sighed a little and said, 'Did you really tell people all that? About being a Duke's daughter?'

'Oh yes. I used to tell the most awful lies. Don't most children? There's usually a reason . . .'

Aunt Alice smiled. With her back to the light and smiling, she looked quite pretty and young, Mary thought. She put out her hand and Aunt Alice took it and turned it over thoughtfully, as if she were going to read the lines on the palm.

'Why did you tell Simon I used to be a nurse?' she asked, so suddenly and unexpectedly, that Mary answered at once.

'To make him fetch you, of course. Because I wanted you to come.'

Aunt Alice sat very still. Then she said, in her bright voice, 'It was just as well I did, wasn't it? Poor little boy.'

'I didn't mean just that,' Mary said. 'I mean I wanted you to come for *me*.'

'Oh,' Aunt Alice said. 'Oh Mary . . .'

Her voice sounded quite different now, and Mary was afraid she was going to cry, so she tugged on her hand to make Aunt Alice come down to kiss her. And when she did, Mary put both arms round her neck and held her tight.

THIRTEEN

The Last Refugee on the Island

WHEN THE FRONT door bell rang, Mary flew out the back way and across the lawn and into the shrubbery. She sat huddled up on the damp, leafy ground, arms wrapped round her knees. She whispered under her breath, 'I'm afraid Mary's not here, anymore. I'm sorry there wasn't time to let you know, and stop you coming. No, we don't know where she's gone. She's quite all right, though, quite safe. She asked me to tell you that, and not to try and find her, because you never will . . .'

It was raining. The rain dripped through the leaves and plopped on top of her head and trickled down her face. She put out her tongue and caught a drop on the end. It tasted salt, like the sea. Or like tears.

She said, 'I'm sorry you had such a long journey for nothing. All this way. But there's no point in waiting. Or in calling her. She won't come . . .'

Aunt Alice said, 'Mary . . .'

She crept into the shrubbery, and crouched on her haunches. Twigs had caught in her hair and tweaked out wisps from her bun. After one look, Mary put her head down on her knees.

'Mary dear,' Aunt Alice said. 'You know who's here?'

Mary pressed down as if she could push herself into the ground and grow roots. Her breath came in short, shallow gasps.

'Please,' Aunt Alice said. She touched Mary's hand.

'I can't,' Mary said. 'I can't ...'

Aunt Alice said nothing.

Mary lifted her head and looked at her. 'I feel sick inside.'

'I know.'

'You could say I wasn't here. Or dead. Or something ...'

'It's no good running away,' Aunt Alice said.

They came out of the shrubbery, across the lawn, and into the house. Mary watched her feet walking. Aunt Alice was just behind her.

There were three people in the room. Grandfather and another man, standing by the window; and her mother on the hearth rug, her hand stretched out to the first fire of the autumn. Rings winked on her fingers.

'Darling,' she said. 'Goodness, you've grown! Quite a beanpole!'

Mary felt clumsy; her arms swung at her sides like weights. She stumped across acres of carpet and stood to be kissed.

'You smell of violets,' she said.

The man by the window laughed.

'*Darling!*' her mother said, and laughed too, as if Mary had said something ridiculous. 'It's a terribly expensive scent!' She put her hands on Mary's shoulders. 'Let me look at you!'

Mary looked at her. She had forgotten how pretty she was—all shining, smooth hair and big, soft eyes—and how young. Too young to be anyone's mother!

The man by the window said, 'I can't believe it. I really can't believe it!' He had a loud, jolly voice.

'True, I'm afraid,' Mary's mother said. 'This really is my *enormous* daughter. And Mary darling, this is *Jeff*. I hope you are going to be great friends.'

'I'm sure we will be.' Jeff came over to the fire. He was tall and good looking, like a man in an advertisement. 'I'm sure we will be,' he repeated, and winked at her. 'Quite a girl, aren't you? I've been reading all about you in the newspapers!'

Aunt Alice said breathlessly, 'I'm so sorry . . . The reporter came to the door and talked to Mary before I could stop him. Actually, I thought he was the gas man. That's why I let her answer the door. It's all my fault.'

'Nonsense, Alice,' Grandfather said. 'It doesn't matter, anyway. Just a nine days wonder . . .'

'I liked being in the paper, Aunt Alice,' Mary said, although in fact she had neither liked nor disliked it. It had simply seemed strange, reading about herself, and Simon, and Krishna. As if they were three people she didn't know at all . . .

'I bet you liked it!' Jeff squeezed her hand. 'I *bet* you did!'

Mary wondered if he always said everything twice, and wished he would let go her hand.

But he went on holding it. 'How's your young friend? Young Patel . . . ?'

'Very well, thank you,' Mary said. 'He had an operation, you know, but he's much better now. We're going to see him this afternoon.'

'I want to hear all about it, sometime. All about it.' Jeff gazed solemnly and steadily into her face, as if he were looking for something.

Mary guessed why he was trying so hard to be nice. She said, 'Are you going to marry my mother?'

Jeff threw back his head and laughed. 'Straight from the shoulder! I like that. I like that *very* much! Yes, Mary, I am.' He released her hand and took her mother's, instead. 'I hope you approve,' he said.

They looked very nice together, Mary thought. Both so

young and smooth, with no pouches or wrinkles in their skin, or creases in their clothes. They made Grandfather and Aunt Alice look rather shabby and crumpled.

Her mother said, 'Darling, I hope it's not *too* much of a surprise! I meant to write before I came, but we've been so dreadfully busy. A hundred and one things to do. Have you heard from Daddy? He promised he'd write, but you know how lazy he is!'

'No. He hasn't written to me,' Mary said. 'Is he coming home?'

She asked out of politeness. She was sure she knew the answer already.

As she did. 'He's staying in South America, darling,' her mother said. 'He likes the climate, he says!' She stopped. 'Darling, *do* take that look off your face. Do you feel very cross?'

'No,' Mary said. It was odd, but she didn't feel anything very much. 'I was just thinking,' she said. 'Are you going to live in the flat?'

Jeff shook his head. 'But we're looking for something very much like it! Convenient and central and with enough room . . .' He winked at Mary's mother, and then at Mary, as if they were all three sharing some tremendously funny joke. 'Enough room for you, if you want to come,' he said.

Mary stared at her feet. 'I don't know.'

'Don't know what, darling?' her mother said.

Mary thought her feet looked unfamiliar, somehow. As if they belonged to someone else. Her voice seemed to belong to someone else too. 'I just don't know.'

Her mother said. 'Of course, we haven't found the right flat, yet. It'll take a little time.'

Mary felt something then: a wave of relief that seemed to rush through her and over her. They weren't going to take her away, then! At least, not now! Not at once!

Her mother said, 'You can come and help us look, if you like. If you want to.'

Mary looked at her. She was smiling her soft, pretty smile, but it looked rather fixed, as if she were posing for a photograph.

Mary thought—Why, she's only being *polite!*

For a moment, there was a queer, suffocating feeling in her throat and she wanted to run away—out of the room, out of the house. Then she looked at Aunt Alice and remembered what she had said in the shrubbery, *it's no good running away*, and knew that it was true. It couldn't change anything, or make any difference: she could run as far and as fast as she liked, but her mother and Jeff and Grampy and Aunt Alice would still be here, in this room, waiting for her answer.

Her mother said, '*Do* you want to, darling?'

It was no good telling lies, either.

Mary said, 'I'd rather stay with Grampy and Aunt Alice, if you don't mind.' And stared at the carpet which was red, with faded orange flowers on it.

Someone in the room let out breath in a long sigh.

Mary looked up. Her mother was still softly smiling, but more naturally than before.

'Of course I don't mind, darling,' she said—and Mary knew that she meant it. 'But we must ask Grampy. And Aunt Alice, of course.'

Mary looked at them.

'Glad to have her. She keeps us lively,' Grandfather said, and blew his nose.

'We've got quite fond of her.' Aunt Alice laughed in the

high, nervous way Mary used to think was so silly. 'Between you and me and the gatepost!' she said.

They all went out to lunch at the big hotel on the front. They had shrimp cocktail and roast chicken with peas and curls of crisp bacon, and lemon sorbet ice, and everyone ate a lot and talked and enjoyed themselves so much that Aunt Alice and Mary were five minutes late at the hospital.

Simon was already there, at Krishna's bedside. Krishna was sitting up in bed in a pair of beautiful, purple pyjamas with a red dragon embroidered on the breast pocket.

'My Uncle brought them,' he said. 'And the grapes, and the books. He is coming again today, because I had my stitches out this morning.'

'Did it hurt?' Mary asked.

'Oh, it was terrible.' Krishna fell back against the pillows and rolled his eyes up, so only the whites showed. 'There were three doctors to hold me down, while another came with a great, sharp knife ...'

'Liar,' Simon said, and helped himself to a grape.

'I was only making it more interesting for Mary. She likes stories.' Krishna giggled, and looked at Mary. 'It was just a tickle, really. Would you like to see my clippings?'

'Your what?'

'Clippings,' Krishna said proudly. 'Newspaper clippings. All about *me*. My Uncle brought them.'

He took an envelope out of his locker and emptied it on the bed. Some of the cuttings were just paragraphs, in small print, but two had photographs: one the reporter had taken of Mary, and another of Simon, which had a headline above it. POLICEMAN'S SON IN RESCUE BID.

'Was your Dad very angry?' Mary said.

'Not as much as I'd expected,' Simon said, and took another grape. 'Mr Patel came to see him.'

Mary glanced at Krishna who was busy showing Aunt Alice the newspaper cuttings. She said, under her breath, 'Was *he* angry?'

She was afraid of meeting Krishna's Uncle. They had kidnapped his nephew, after all . . .

Simon shook his head. 'Not when I saw him.' He spat grape pips into his hand and looked shyly at Mary. 'I was wrong,' he said.

'What about?'

'Oh. Just about things. Where he lived, for one . . .' He blushed; then grinned. 'But I was right about the Cadillac! He hasn't got one!' He looked at Mary triumphantly and leaned forward to take another grape. 'Only a Rolls Royce,' he said.

'What are you whispering about?' Krishna said, and then, in the same breath, 'Here is my Uncle.'

Mary looked. A dark gentleman was walking down the ward. He wasn't very tall, and he had a delicate, narrow face, very like Krishna's. He kissed Krishna; shook hands with Aunt Alice and Simon, then with Mary. 'So this is your other gallant friend!' he said.

'Mary,' Krishna said. 'She pulls awfully good faces.'

Uncle Patel smiled at her. 'I have to thank you for taking such good care of my nephew. He was fortunate to fall into such kind hands.'

Mary felt pleased, and terribly embarrassed.

Krishna said, 'Pull some faces now, Mary. Pull the mad face!'

Mary shook her head.

'But I *want* you to!' Krishna said.

'I can't. Not here.'

'It's not Church,' Aunt Alice said.

Mary thought they were all looking at her as if it was mean of her to refuse what Krishna wanted, so she did her best. Aunt Alice shuddered and closed her eyes, but Krishna laughed and then clutched his stomach and said, 'No! Stop! Don't make me laugh, it hurts my scar . . .' Tears came into his eyes and his Uncle took his hand.

'Well, you did *ask*.' Mary felt she had been put in the wrong. She looked crossly at Aunt Alice who smiled, and winked at her privately.

Aunt Alice said, 'We ought to go now, dear. Krishna mustn't get too excited.'

Krishna pouted and thumped up and down in the bed. 'Don't go. I don't want any of you to go.'

'Hush, my lamb,' Aunt Alice said—but severely, as if she thought Krishna had had his own way quite long enough.

He lay still then, and looked at her with his plum-coloured eyes. 'But we haven't had a proper talk yet! About the island! Have you been back, Simon?'

'I'm going this afternoon to fetch my camping gear.'

'*I* want to go,' Krishna said. 'It's not *fair*.'

Uncle Patel was smiling. 'There will be plenty of time when you are well. I have heard this morning that you will be allowed to stay with me until your parents come, which should not be too long, I think.' He looked at Aunt Alice. 'There has been a lot of interest shown in Krishna's case. Our young friends have had something to do with that, I think. The publicity has been useful! And also the fact that they hid him, of course! The longer you can remain in the country without being caught, the better your chance of being allowed to stay!'

Mary looked at Krishna, to see if he had appreciated all

they had done for him, but he seemed not to be listening to his Uncle, just waiting for him to stop speaking. When he did, Krishna caught Aunt Alice's hand and burst out, 'There is a thing I have been thinking about. Simon's Uncle fetched me in a boat. Where did it come from? All the time we were there, we did not see a boat. Nor any people, either.'

'Didn't you ever go beyond the bridge, my lambkin?' Aunt Alice said.

She looked at Simon, smiled mysteriously, and bent to whisper in Krishna's ear.

'What did she mean? Why didn't she tell *me*?' Mary said, when they got to the island.

'I suppose she thought I'd like to show you.'

Simon sighed. He had been very silent ever since they had left the hospital, but although Mary had noticed this, it had not troubled her much. She had been silent herself; her mind too busy to speak.

Now, as Simon led the way further round the lake, she said, 'You heard what Uncle Patel said? About people being allowed to stay in England if they manage not to be caught for a while? Well—we could do it *again*. I mean, we could watch on the beach, and meet immigrants coming in, and bring them to the island and hide them and feed them . . .

'Oh, for God's sake!' Simon stopped so suddenly that she bumped into him. 'Who d'you think you are? James Bond or something?' He looked at her coldly for a minute, and then went on, more kindly, 'They wouldn't have let him stay if he'd been a poor boy, don't you know that? It's just because he's got a rich uncle. I know Mr Patel *said* that about us being helpful, but he was just being nice! As if we were kids who'd been naughty and needed cheering up! Besides, we couldn't hide anyone on the island, not now everyone *knows*. It's not private anymore.' He stopped and swallowed with a rasping sound as if he had something sharp caught in his throat. 'It never was, really . . .'

He turned his back on Mary, and went on. At first the path was no different from the track before the bridge, mossy and damp and overgrown, but after a little it opened out and became firmer underfoot, as if other people had walked there. Then they turned a bend and saw the end of the lake: a broad, shining stretch of water, clear of weed, with a landing stage and several boats moored beside it. On the far bank, well-spaced out as if they didn't care for each other's company, several fishermen sat, with rugs over their knees. And beyond, through the trees, the afternoon sun glinted on metal. Cars in a car park.

'It's a private fishing club,' Simon said in a distant voice. 'A very expensive one. Rich people come down from London. There's another entrance to the estate and a club where the old house used to be. I suppose the reason we never saw them, down our end of the lake, is the weed. I mean, you can't fish there, except for the clear patch, round the island. And they wouldn't bother to walk so far, anyway. Not rich men with cars. But they've been *here*, all the time . . .'

He hunched his shoulders and dug his hands deep into his pockets and scowled fiercely.

Mary watched him for a minute, standing and scowling at the fishermen on the opposite side of the lake.

She said, 'Simon.'

He didn't answer. The fishermen sat so still they might have been stuffed. Only their coloured floats moved, drifting gently with the movement of the water.

Mary said, 'We can't see them from the island. And they can't see us. So it doesn't make any difference. We can pretend they're not there.'

'Pretending's no good,' Simon said. 'What we had before was *real*.'

And he pushed past Mary and began to run back towards the island, so fast that she couldn't keep up with him.

She found him on the bluff above the grotto. He was standing, looking out over the lake. There were tear streaks, like snail tracks, on his face. He gave an affected start, as if he hadn't expected to see her here.

'What are you going to do about Noakes?' he said, as if practical things like this were all they had to talk about.

'I might take him home with me,' Mary said. 'Aunt Alice said I could if I liked.'

'He's wild now,' Simon said. 'He won't stay.'

'*I'm* staying,' Mary said, and felt very happy. So happy that she didn't mind when Simon just said, in an uninterested voice, 'Well, that's different, you're not a wild cat,' and turned to stare out over the lake again.

She said, 'Do cheer up, Simon.'

'I'm all right,' he said, not sounding it. Then he looked at her. 'If you take Noakes home, he'll only run away first chance he gets and try to get back to the island. But even if he finds his way here, he won't be able to cross the bridge because he can't balance with three legs. And then' he'll *die*. He'll die of grief . . .'

He sounded as if he knew what this would feel like.

Mary said, 'Well, I suppose we'd better leave him, then.' She knew it, really: Noakes would never settle in a house, never sit by a fire and grow old and lazy and fat. Not now he had tasted freedom. She said, 'We could always come now and again, to make sure he's all right.'

Silence. A fish plopped in the lake. Then another.

Simon said, 'It won't be the same, of course.'

Mary felt impatient. 'Well, it wasn't the same when *we* came, was it? Krishna and me. I mean, you had the island to yourself before. But it was nice when we *did* come, too. Wasn't it? I mean, things change all the time and it isn't always *sad*. I'm going to look for Noakes now, and you can come if you like, and you can stay if you like, but I'm going.'

'All right, keep your hair on,' Simon said, and turned to her, grinning.

They didn't find Noakes. They didn't see him until they had given up looking and had lit a fire and heated up the last of the sardines in the billy can. Then, when the fire was burning low and the light beginning to fade on the lake, he appeared on the edge of the bluff and played with a leaf, rushing and pouncing with little snarls of mock anger. He wouldn't let them touch him but stayed close while they packed up and stamped out the fire and then followed them to the bridge, keeping his distance and growling softly.

When they had crossed to the mainland, Mary looked back. Noakes was watching them, still growling and switching his tail, but she thought he looked, suddenly, not wild at all but rather lonely and lost; the last refugee on the island ...

'I hate leaving him,' she said, speaking softly, to herself, but Simon heard her.

'If you took him, he'd hate it *more!* And we're not leaving him, really. We can come back.'

Mary looked at him. The sun, slanting low over the trees, shone in his eyes and made them shimmer, like water.

'We can come back *tomorrow*,' Simon said.

And on the island, Noakes gave one last twitch of his tail and leapt into the bushes, out of their sight.